Her attraction to hi
Something she could
She'd been fighting a losing battle sin
she'd arrived in town.

The battle to resist him.

"You're good at this, aren't you?" she asked.

"Good at what?"

"Good at being so darn irresistible," she admitted.

There. She'd said it. She couldn't deny it any longer, and she didn't want to. The truth was, she wanted Aaron. She wanted a taste of him again. Maybe then she could fully get him out of her system.

"You find me irresistible?" His eyes lighting up, he drew his bottom lip between his teeth, indicating to her that he knew just how enticing he was.

"You're good at making a woman weak with need," Melissa said softly. "Good at making her want you."

"Baby, you ain't seen nothing yet."

The words were a promise. A promise that Melissa wanted him to fulfill.

One night with Aaron… It wasn't something she'd ever imagined before she'd arrived in Sheridan Falls, but right now she wanted nothing more.

Dear Reader,

When I was young, a family at my church consisted of three brothers. What is it about a group of brothers that makes them instantly more appealing? These boys were infamous. All the guys wanted to be like them, and the girls wanted to date them.

I was one of those girls. I liked the taller, cuter one. He was my first crush, my first kiss. Then came devastation when his parents split and he, his brothers and his mother moved a few thousand miles away.

No one ever forgot them. And I certainly never forgot the excitement of falling in love for the first time. It's the same excitement my heroine, Melissa, experiences when she falls for the popular Aaron Burke.

The definite appeal of more than one brother is that there are more you might have a chance with. Here there are four. Welcome to the world of the Burke brothers!

Kayla

Undeniable Attraction

Kayla Perrin

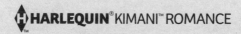
HARLEQUIN® KIMANI™ ROMANCE

Recycling programs
for this product may
not exist in your area.

ISBN-13: 978-1-335-21674-8

Undeniable Attraction

For questions and comments about the quality of this book please contact us at CustomerService@Harlequin.com.

Printed in U.S.A.

Kayla Perrin is a multi-award-winning, multipublished *USA TODAY* and *Essence* bestselling author. She's been writing since she could hold a pencil, and sent her first book to a publisher when she was just thirteen years old. Since 1998, she's had over fifty novels and novellas published. She's been featured in *Ebony* magazine, *RT Book Reviews*, *South Florida Business Journal*, the *Toronto Star* and other Canadian and US publications. Her works have been translated into Italian, German, Spanish and Portuguese. In 2011, Kayla received the prestigious Harry Jerome Award for excellence in the arts in Canada. She lives in the Toronto area with her daughter. You can find Kayla on Facebook, Twitter and Instagram. Please visit her website at authorkaylaperrin.com.

Books by Kayla Perrin

Harlequin Kimani Romance

Taste of Desire
Always in My Heart
Surrender My Heart
Heart to Heart
Until Now
Burning Desire
Flames of Passion
Passion Ignited
Sizzling Desire
Undeniable Attraction

Visit the Author Profile page
at Harlequin.com for more titles.

For May-Marie Duwa-Sowi,
founder of *Illuminessence* magazine.
Your vision is extraordinary and awe inspiring.
I know your big dreams are about to come true.
I'm proud to call you a friend and say, "I knew you when."
Keep illuminating!

Chapter 1

Sheridan Falls, 10 Miles

Melissa Conwell's hands tightened on the steering wheel as she passed the familiar sign along Interstate 90 west. Sheridan Falls. She was almost home.

Home home. Not Newark, New Jersey, where she lived now, but the small town in upstate New York where she'd been born and raised. Normally, seeing that sign caused her heart to fill with happiness, knowing that she would soon be seeing her parents, sister and young niece. But today, the fact that she was almost home had her throat tightening.

It was an illogical reaction, especially since she was returning to Sheridan Falls for a joyous occasion. It was sure to be *the* event of the summer, a big wedding that was bringing family members together from across the country. And yet joy was the last thing she was feeling.

She was anxious. Terrified, even.

Because this time she was going to have to see Aaron Burke. Small-town boy turned international soccer star.

International heartbreaker, more like.

She hadn't needed to read the tabloids to learn that Aaron had had his share of women and had broken his share of hearts. She knew that from firsthand experience. Eleven years, nine months and ten or so days ago, Aaron had crushed her teenage heart and left her reeling.

Not that she was counting or anything.

Melissa's fingers began to hurt, and she loosened her grip on the steering wheel. Why she was getting all tense at the thought of seeing Aaron was beyond her. She hadn't spoken to him in nearly twelve years. He wasn't part of her life, by any stretch of the imagination. So why was she acting as if seeing him was going to disrupt her world?

Because she didn't *want* to see him. Ever. Not after how things had ended between them. She might be over him, but they weren't friends, and spending time with him was going to be awkward at the very least.

But that's exactly what she was going to have to do. Over the next few days, she was going to be seeing a lot of Aaron—at the welcome dinner, at the rehearsal, at the wedding. And worse than simply seeing him, she was going to have to interact and play nice, because not only was Melissa in the wedding party, Aaron was, too. And for some unfathomable reason, Tasha had paired Aaron with her.

"What's the big deal?" Tasha had asked when Melissa expressed mortification over the wedding arrangements. "The other pairings made more sense this way. Besides, you and Aaron used to be close."

"Exactly—*used* to be," Melissa had said. "We haven't spoken in years. Are you forgetting what he did to me?"

"But weren't you the one who decided not to follow him to Notre Dame?" Tasha asked, sounding confused. "You said he'd be too busy with his soccer scholarship and you didn't want to get in his way? Then things fell apart after that."

Melissa had been glad that she and her cousin were speaking on the phone, three thousand miles between them. Because she didn't want Tasha to see her face.

The story that Melissa was the one who'd decided not to go to Notre Dame had not been entirely truthful, but it had been much better than admitting that Aaron had rejected her. She'd been trying to save face when she'd told her close friends and family that she was the one who'd chosen not to follow Aaron to college. The truth was, Aaron had been the one to ask her why she would travel across the country for school when there were better social work programs closer to home. Melissa had been stunned. Didn't he *want* her around? Didn't he love her?

Melissa's heart had been beating out of control as Tasha

had gone on to talk about how Melissa being paired with Aaron would be fine, that years had passed and she was sure there would be no tension between them. Melissa hoped her cousin was right, but she wouldn't bet money on it. How did you play nice with someone you'd tried to eradicate from your memory?

Melissa gazed out at the familiar landscape. The trees along the interstate were a vibrant green and in full bloom. The sky was cloudless and a gorgeous cerulean blue this early-summer day. The weather for the weekend was supposed to be perfect.

If only she could feel good about it.

Her mind ventured back to the one thing she couldn't escape—the fact that she would have to see Aaron. Did she hate him? No, hate was too strong an emotion, but she certainly didn't like him. Once she'd learned that Aaron had done the unthinkable—he'd married Ella Donovan, the one girl in high school she couldn't stand—any remaining respect she might have had for him instantly died. He'd given Melissa the song and dance about how they were young, it was time for them to concentrate on their careers, that the distance between them would eventually become a factor.

Yet somehow he'd ended up making a relationship work with Ella? Ella had stayed in Sheridan Falls and worked for her father, who'd been the longtime mayor of the town. When had Aaron had time to forge a relationship with her?

Unless they'd been involved while he and Melissa had been. Every unthinkable scenario had crossed Melissa's mind, and she'd ultimately been livid with herself for falling for a Burke brother. Hadn't she known better? During high school, she'd heard all the rumors about the four Burke boys, how they dated whomever they wanted, were too popular to be faithful and women were supposed to take what they could get—*if* they were lucky enough to catch the eye of one of the Burkes. Which was exactly why Melissa had always vowed to never be like the other women in town, who seemed to lose their minds whenever in the presence of Aaron, Keith, Carlton or Jonas. Yes, the Burkes were hot, but it was pathetic how googly-eyed women became around them.

And then Melissa spent a summer with Aaron. They were both hired by a local camp at the end of their senior high school year as counselors charged with entertaining kids twelve and under. Melissa and Aaron had spent a lot of time together, time in which she'd gotten to know him. And he'd seemed so different from everything she'd heard. Caring. Funny. Engaging. Truly interested in the kids. Relatable. A good listener. He didn't seem conceited at all. And somehow, Melissa had fallen for him.

Her first love. Her first heartbreak.

Dreams shattered. Her innocence lost.

The best summer of her life had turned into her biggest regret.

Though Melissa had tried to the best of her ability to avoid following Aaron's career and his life over the years, she hadn't been able to avoid everything. She had seen the photos of him in various highlights on the news about his soccer achievements, and of course about his happy marriage to the mayor's daughter.

It was rare that she didn't find a story about Aaron whenever she looked up news in the online version of the *Sheridan Falls Tribune*. In their town of seven thousand people, Aaron Burke was a local hero. Even him buying a new car made the paper.

Melissa had fallen for him before he'd ever become successful, though he had always been legendary. He was the son of Cyrus Burke, a local celebrity who'd had a long and celebrated career in the NFL. Not that Melissa knew anything about Cyrus's personal life, but every time she'd seen him in town with his wife, Cynthia, he seemed like a man in love. Always holding her hand. Opening doors for her. Gazing at her fondly, as though there was no woman more beautiful in the world.

There'd never been a hint of scandal about Cyrus's fidelity, something Melissa had reflected on after she and Aaron had become an item. She'd figured like father, like son, and had assumed that if Aaron became successful as a soccer player, he would be like his father. Instead, he'd proceeded to behave exactly like the majority of highly paid professional athletes out there—parties, women, a string of broken hearts.

Melissa had read all about it in the tabloids. Seen pictures of him on yachts in the Mediterranean with other soccer players and a horde of bikini-clad women. She'd seen how female sports reporters would look up at him with the same googly eyes she'd witnessed on the women from Sheridan Falls. It had been hard for Melissa to stomach.

And then Aaron had married Ella in some big event in Sheridan Falls, and Melissa had stopped paying attention to what Aaron did with his life. She'd spent too much time over the years thinking about him as it was, and if he could marry the one person who'd made her life hell in high school, he didn't deserve a second thought.

"Enough of this nonsense," she said to herself. Vowing to forget about Aaron, she turned up the music on the radio and bopped her head to an upbeat tune. Her eyes ventured to the lake as she crossed the city limits into Sheridan Falls. That was the lake on which she'd spent her last summer of high school as a counselor.

The summer she had fallen in love with Aaron Burke.

"Oh, for goodness' sake," she all but yelled. "Stop thinking about Aaron! He's ancient history."

Suddenly, it hit her what the real issue was. She didn't want to see him with Ella, who she knew would rub in the fact that she had snagged a Burke brother. Having to stom-

ach Ella gloating over her coveted prize would be more
than Melissa could bear. In high school, Ella had lived to
steal other women's men, as though it were a competitive
sport. If only Aaron had ended up with anyone but her.
Ella, who'd never suffered from self-esteem issues to begin
with, must have an ego as large as the state of Texas now.

Dealing with Ella's gloating would be bearable *if* Melissa were heading home with a hot man on her arm. But
sadly, she was single. Her relationships over the years had
all died before any real promise of a happily-ever-after. Her
most recent relationship had started off with hope, in part
because of the fact that Christopher worked in the social
work field, as did she. But hope had faded as quickly as
the initial spark, and the relationship had ended without
so much as a fizzle.

"You don't need to return home with a man," Melissa
said. "All you have to do is ignore Aaron. Pretend like he
doesn't exist."

Because he didn't. He hadn't existed in her life for over
a decade, and that wasn't about to change just because of
the wedding.

Chapter 2

A slow smile spread on Melissa's lips as she pulled into the driveway of her parents' home, the house in which she had been born and raised. Gone were all thoughts of Aaron as she saw her mother sitting on the porch swing. As Melissa exited her navy Chevrolet Malibu, her mother got to her feet, her eyes lighting up with excitement.

"Melissa!" her mother exclaimed. "Ooh, come here, child."

Melissa quickly closed the car door and rushed up the porch steps. Her mother's arms were already spread wide, and Melissa threw herself into her embrace. Her mom hugged her long and hard against her large bosom. Instantly, Melissa felt a sense of comfort, the same way she always had as a little girl when her mother had wrapped her in her arms.

The weekend was going to be okay. Why had she been worrying herself silly?

"My baby." Her mother broke the hug, leaned backward to check her out and took both of Melissa's hands in hers. "Looks like you could use some good home cooking. You're getting a little thin."

Her mother had grown up in the South, and practically everything she made had a stick of butter or lard in it. It was a diet Melissa tried to steer clear of, for the most part. "I've been working out."

"I'll get some meat back on your bones," her mother promised. Then she said, "It has been way too long since you've been home. It's like you've forgotten your father and me now that you're living in the big city."

"You know I could never forget about you and Dad," Melissa said. She squeezed her mother's hands affectionately, then released them. "I meant to come back after Christmas, but I've been so busy with work."

"Some days I wonder about that job of yours."

"I love it," Melissa said quickly, walking into the house. "Even the crazy hours and the emergencies." Being the program coordinator at a group home in Newark was deeply rewarding. Melissa made an impact in the lives of troubled youth, helping the kids get back on track.

"I know your job is important. But I don't like that you have to devote so much time to it. All work and no play, you'll never find a nice man."

Melissa offered her mother a small smile, though what she wanted to do was roll her eyes. Her mother would never be fully happy until Melissa had been married off.

Though her mom should know by now that marriage didn't mean happiness. Her sister, Arlene, had just endured a nasty divorce. Her parents had viewed Craig as the son they'd never had, only to be devastated when he'd turned his back on not only Arlene, but also on them. He'd cheated with his secretary, then had the nerve to be unapologetic about his actions. The ensuing scandal had caused much embarrassment for Arlene and the family.

"Where's Dad?"

"He's lying down," her mother said, and now she was the one to roll her eyes. "The crazy fool tired himself out retiling the basement bathroom. I told him to hire someone, but *no*, he swore he could do it himself. I think he threw his back out, but he'll never admit it."

Oh, yes. Melissa was home, all right. Her parents always bickered, sometimes from sunup until sundown, but despite their small disagreements, their deep love was never in doubt.

"I'm about ready to tell him that if he doesn't call in a professional, I'm leaving him. This time I mean it."

Melissa chortled. "Mom, you know you're not going

anywhere. You always threaten to leave, but you never will. And you know why? Because you and Dad would be lost without each other."

Melissa crossed through the living room en route to her parents' bedroom. She found her father lying in bed, his eyes closed, but when he heard her, he opened them and immediately smiled.

"Melissa," he said warmly, starting to sit up.

Melissa hurried over to him. "No, Dad. Don't get up. Mom said you threw your back out."

Her father made a face and waved a dismissive hand. "I'm fine. Ripping out tile is hard work. I just needed a little nap, is all."

"You didn't pull your back out?"

"Of course not," he scoffed, his tone saying the idea was ridiculous. But he winced after speaking the words.

Melissa leaned down and hugged her father, then sat on the edge of the bed. "It's good to see you, Dad."

"It's always good to see my favorite daughter."

"And what do you say to Arlene?" Melissa asked, raising an eyebrow in a feigned gesture of seriousness.

"That she's my favorite, too. A father is allowed to have two favorites."

"Only two?" Melissa asked.

"Two favorite children. And numerous favorite grandchildren."

"Hmm, that's convenient," Melissa said. Then she grinned down at her dad. "I love you." She got up off the bed. "You need anything?"

"I'd tell you to get me a beer, but your mother is watching me like a hawk. She thinks if I cut down on beer, my belly will disappear."

"How about water?" Melissa suggested.

"How about a new wife?" her father shot back.

"Sure. Should I go into town and pick one up for you?

Bringing her home could be tough, though. It could get ugly with Mom."

"I'll have some water," her father said grudgingly.

Melissa smirked, then exited the bedroom. She heard her cell phone ringing and quickly ran to the front of the house, where she'd dropped her purse. Seconds later, she had her phone in her hand and saw her sister's smiling face flashing on the screen.

"Hey, sis," Melissa greeted her.

"You here?" Arlene asked without preamble. "In Sheridan Falls?"

"Yep. Just got to Mom and Dad's."

"Great. We need you here ASAP."

A loud wail sounded in the background. "Where are you?" Melissa asked. "And what is going on?"

"We're at the bridal shop," Arlene told her. "Tasha is having a meltdown. She's worried your dress won't fit, and there's only a short time left for alterations. Tasha's maid of honor put on ten pounds and her dress has to be altered."

"I'm sure my dress will be fine," Melissa said. "I sent in my exact measurements for every part of my body, and my weight hasn't changed. I might have lost a couple of pounds, actually."

"Yeah, well, nothing's going to appease Tasha unless she sees it with her own eyes. How quickly can you get here?"

"I'm on my way."

Melissa arrived at the upscale bridal shop twelve minutes later and found the bridal party in the back. Tasha was slumped in a velour armchair, two of her bridesmaids on either side of her. Maxine, Tasha's older sister, stood to her right and held Tasha's hand. The friend who must be Tasha's maid of honor was on her knees beside the chaise. She was also holding Tasha's hand and worrying her bottom lip.

"How can you tell me everything will be all right, Maxine?" Tasha demanded. "Bonnie's dress doesn't fit. And she's my maid of honor. She has to look amazing."

Tasha shot a glance at the woman on her knees. Yes, she was definitely Bonnie. "It's only the zipper," Bonnie said. Her plump face lit up with a reassuring smile. "Enid already said that can be fixed. Plus, I'll eat only salad for the next two days."

"But what about Melissa?" Tasha countered. "What if her dress doesn't fi—"

Tasha's words died on her lips as her eyes ventured beyond the women trying to console her and landed on Melissa. Tasha immediately eased up in the chair. "Melissa?"

"Hey, you." Melissa beamed as she moved toward her cousin. The moment Tasha got to her feet, Melissa took her in her arms.

"You're here," Tasha said, then burst into tears.

"Hey," Melissa said softly, easing back and taking Tasha's hands in hers. "What's this all about?"

"I just want everything to be perfect, and if your dress doesn't fit…maybe they won't get all the alterations done in time."

"It'll fit," Melissa assured her.

The attendant, a red-haired woman with a worried expression on her face, whom Melissa had briefly noticed as she entered she shop, tentatively approached the group. "I'm Enid." She looked Melissa directly in the eye. "I take it you're Melissa."

"Yes."

"Oh, thank God." The woman's shoulders slumped with relief.

Melissa fully turned to face the woman, asking, "Where's my dress?"

"It's hanging in dressing room number four." Enid pointed toward the door. "You can try it on any time you're ready." Then she leaned close to Melissa and whispered, "But sooner would be better."

"Got it," Melissa said, facing her cousin and giving her a bright smile. "Everything's going to be okay. Don't you worry."

Tasha nodded, but her glum expression said she didn't believe Melissa's mollifying words.

Melissa greeted the other women with smiles and hellos, then briefly hugged her sister before heading into the dressing room. The bridesmaid dress was hanging on the back of the door. Melissa's eyes widened as she checked it out. It looked even more beautiful in person than it had in photos. The lavender dress was a floor-length, one-shoulder stunner. The charmeuse fabric was soft and shimmery. The bodice of the dress was covered with a layer of lace, and a ribbon of satin surrounded the dress's waist.

A lump of emotion suddenly formed in Melissa's throat. She'd always thought that by thirty, she would either be married or on her way to being married. Yet here she was, single with no prospects, while her twenty-seven-year-old cousin had found the love of her life.

Melissa disrobed and put the dress on. It was meant to be fitted from the waist up and flowed elegantly from the waist down. There was a slit in the dress that came to midthigh.

"Do you need any help?" the attendant asked.

Melissa opened the door. "If you could zip me up…"

The attendant eased forward and zipped the dress at the back, then Melissa fully exited the dressing room and moved to stand in front of the floor-to-ceiling mirror. The rest of the bridesmaids gathered around her. Through the mirror, Melissa could see their eyes lighting up. That was when she fully took note of her outfit, giving it a slow gaze from the top of the one shoulder, along the lace-covered bodice that somehow managed to make her breasts look more shapely, and down to the length of the flowing skirt. A smile spread on her face. It fit her perfectly. And she looked beautiful.

Tasha came up behind her, and her eyes filled with fresh tears. She had already cried a lot, given how puffy and red her eyes were. But at least these tears were happy ones.

A bubble of laughter escaped Tasha's throat. "It's perfect. You look gorgeous. Just stunning."

"I told you not to worry," Melissa said.

"You look so beautiful."

Melissa turned and faced her cousin, the gown swooshing around her bare feet. "But not nearly as beautiful as you'll be. The picture you sent me of you in your dress… you're going to knock Ryan off his feet."

"You think so?" Tasha asked, a hitch in her voice.

"I know so." Melissa reached out and tucked a strand of her cousin's curly hair behind her ear. "How could you not?"

Tasha beamed. "Everything's going to be fine, isn't it?"

"Of course it is," Melissa said. "Why wouldn't it be? You're marrying the love of your life, and he absolutely adores you. Everything is going to be perfect."

Tasha wiped at her eyes. "You're right." Then she glanced at the rest of the bridal party. "I'm sorry I've been such an emotional mess."

Maxine looped an arm through her sister's. "You've just got the prewedding jitters. It's perfectly normal."

"But Bonnie's dress—" Tasha said.

"Will be fine," Enid said, stepping forward. "There's enough room to let the dress out at the sides so that it zips up. I'll be working as long as necessary to make sure that everything is just right."

Tasha inhaled and exhaled deeply. "You've been so good to me, Enid. Working overtime to make sure that all is perfect."

"I'm happy that you gave our boutique the opportunity,"

Enid said, smiling. "A big wedding like yours... I thought for sure you'd find a boutique in Buffalo or New York City."

"Never," Tasha said. "You and I go way back. Fourth grade. Of course I'd give you the business." She squeezed Enid's hands, then glanced at her wristwatch. "Ooh, we only have a couple of hours before the welcome dinner. We should really get out of here so we can get ready."

Melissa glanced at Enid, seeing relief wash over her face. "The alterations will be started immediately," she said in an effort to allay any possible concerns that Tasha might have.

Melissa waved a dismissive hand. "No worries. We'll be back tomorrow for the dresses."

Tasha wandered back over to the armchair where she'd been sitting, lifted the champagne glass from the table beside it and finished off the contents. "Okay, ladies. My meltdown is over. Let's get ready for tonight's dinner."

Chapter 3

Tasha was marrying Ryan Burke, part of the Burke family dynasty in Sheridan Falls. He was Aaron's first cousin, which explained why Aaron—and his brothers—were in the wedding party.

Melissa slowed her car as she approached the sprawling house where the welcome dinner was to be held. The Burke estate.

She had never been there before, but she'd driven past it when she was a teenager. She and her friends had marveled at the mansion where the town's most famous family lived.

The Burke home was in an exclusive neighborhood in the city's west end. There were only three homes on this court, and the Burkes' house, in the center of the court, was the largest. It was arguably the largest house in town.

Though Ryan was Cynthia and Cyrus Burke's nephew, the welcome dinner was being held at their home because of its large size, plus its location on the lake, which made it an ideal spot.

Melissa pulled up behind a silver Lexus SUV. Her pulse was racing as she exited her car and made her way to the massive cobblestone driveway leading to the house. It was a Georgian colonial-style home with a gray stone and white wood exterior. There were two stately pillars standing on each side of the red front door, which provided a pop of color in the center of the house. The four pillars held up a rectangular balcony on the second floor.

There was a circular fountain in the center of the driveway, around which was a bed of colorful flowers. A myriad of luxury cars filled the space. Mercedes sedans and SUVs. BMWs. A classic Corvette was parked at the front of the house, before the main door. Canary yellow. That was Cyrus's vehicle. Melissa remembered him driving around in that sports car when she was young. The paint was shiny and polished, and there wasn't a blemish on it. If she hadn't known it was an older car, she would've thought it was brand-new.

Melissa counted approximately thirteen cars in the driveway, not including the ones parked on the street. The place was clearly packed. There were more people here than she'd expected for a welcome dinner, but she'd heard that the extended Burke family was vast.

Melissa took her time heading up to the house, acutely aware of the fact that she would be seeing Aaron any minute now. She wished more than anything that she had a man on her arm. It was silly, she knew. But she wished she could look outrageously happy with a gorgeous and affectionate man when she saw Aaron for the first time in years.

"You have nothing to prove to him," she told herself as she made her way along the stone path that led to the front door.

She could hear music coming from the back of the house and hoped that someone would be able to hear the door. She rang the doorbell and waited.

Less than a minute later, a man dressed in a black suit, white shirt and black bow tie answered the door. "Good afternoon," he said, greeting her with a warm smile.

"Hello," Melissa responded. "I'm here for the party."

"Of course. Take this hallway on the right, then take a left when you reach the kitchen. When you walk through the kitchen, you'll see the patio doors that lead to the backyard."

"Thank you." Melissa made her way to the right, following the instructions. She looked around in awe at the vivid paintings of landscapes on the walls, along with some African-inspired art, and wondered what it was like to live this kind of life. Everything about the house was grandiose. From the double staircase in the home's entryway to the wainscoting on the walls and the absolutely massive kitchen filled with gray-and-black marble, this place was absolutely gorgeous, and immaculately decorated.

To their credit, Cynthia and Cyrus Burke did not seem pretentious, even though they were clearly living the dream.

Melissa passed staff in the kitchen preparing trays of hors d'oeuvres. The waiter pouring champagne into flutes caught her eye, and she offered him a smile before continuing on to the patio doors, where she paused and looked outside. She exhaled softly.

Wow.

She stood with her hand on the doorknob, taking it all in. Just outside the doors was a massive deck. Palm trees— yes, palm trees—stood in all corners of the deck, providing a contrast to the white wood. The tree trunks were decked out in strings of tiny white lights. Happy people congregated on the deck, drinks and plates of appetizers in hand.

Melissa opened the door and stepped outside. She made her way to the back of the deck, where a staircase led to the lawn below. The yard was massive. There was no other word to describe it. The lawn extended for at least a couple hundred yards, where it ended at the lake. There was a dock there, with a pleasure boat moored to it. Melissa remembered that years ago when they'd watched his parents cruising on the lake one summer day, Aaron had said the boat was a Boston Whaler.

A huge white tent was set up in the middle of the backyard, and inside it Melissa could see tables and chairs. Just within the entrance to the tent was a table with a giant silver punch bowl, from which punch was flowing as if it were a fountain. Well-dressed people were mingling outside the tent, some inside. Classical music played through the speakers, creating a lovely ambience.

Melissa started down the steps. Most of the people here she either didn't know or hadn't seen in years. Where were the members of the bridal party?

And then she spotted Carlton Burke, Aaron's older brother. He was walking across the lawn on the far right side of the tent with a couple of other people. Melissa swallowed.

"Hello, there."

At the sound of the warm female voice behind her, Melissa turned. She saw Cynthia Burke, wearing a simple white dress with flowing sleeves, moving toward her with the grace of an angel.

"Is that you, Melissa?" Cynthia continued, her eyes lighting up. "All grown up?"

Melissa smiled at the friendly face she hadn't seen in years. "Yes, Mrs. Burke. It's me. How are you?"

Cynthia pulled her into an impromptu hug. "It's so good to see you again." Releasing her, she took Melissa's hand in both of hers. "My, you've grown up so much since your days working with Aaron as a camp counselor."

"Yes, ma'am," Melissa said.

"I'm so glad you're here." Cynthia beamed as she released her hand. Then she looked up at the sky. "And I'm very happy that the weather cooperated for this dinner."

"Yes, it's a beautiful day," Melissa agreed, glancing around. She felt an odd sensation and knew that it was the fear of seeing Aaron. He could appear at any moment, and she wasn't prepared for that.

"Help yourself to some punch," Cynthia said, pointing toward the tent. "Or if you'd like something from the bar, you can get a drink right there." She gestured behind her to the left. There was a patio area along the entire back of the house, complete with a number of white wrought iron tables and chairs. A full-service bar was set up. Two bartenders, a man and a woman, were busy making drinks.

The walk-out lower level of the house boasted floor-to-ceiling windows, and Melissa could only imagine how lovely it was to wake up each morning and start your day with a cup of tea or coffee while enjoying the view here.

"Thank you," she said to Cynthia. "I think I will get a drink."

Just as she spoke the words, the waiter she'd seen in the kitchen filling champagne flutes appeared. He extended the tray, and Melissa took a glass.

Slowly, Melissa walked in the direction of the lake, continuing to survey the massive property. Every tree on the property also had angel lights wrapped around the trunk. There was the fragrant scent of roses in the air, coming from several strategically placed pots filled with lavender-colored roses, which matched the color scheme for the wedding.

In the distance, the lake shimmered beneath the sun's rays. The beauty of this place was breathtaking. It would be a perfect spot for the wedding, if Tasha and Ryan had wanted to have it here.

Melissa took a sip of her champagne and gazed out at the lake again. In the distance, there were other homes that backed onto it. The lake bent and veered to the right a few hundred feet in the distance, and it was around that bend that the campground was.

The camp where Melissa and Aaron had worked as counselors the summer they'd fallen in love.

Well, *she* had fallen in love with him. She doubted that Aaron had ever been in love with her.

She sipped more champagne, needing something to help take the edge off her nerves. No matter how pleasant the view and the music, Melissa hated that she had to be here at the Burke residence right now. She wished she could skip this welcome dinner, but that wasn't an option.

"This is certainly going to be one interesting weekend," she muttered.

"It sure is."

A jolt hit Melissa's body with the force of a soccer ball slamming into her chest. That voice... A tingling sensation spread across her shoulder blades. It was a voice she hadn't heard in a long time. Deeper than she remembered, but it most definitely belonged to *him*.

Holding her breath, she turned. And there he was. Aaron Burke. Looking down at her with a smile on his face and a teasing glint in his eyes.

"I thought that was you," he said, his smile deepening.

Melissa stood there looking up at him from wide eyes, unsure what to say. Why was he grinning at her as though he was happy to see her?

"It's good to see you, Melissa."

Aaron spread his arms wide, an invitation. But Melissa stood still, as if paralyzed. With a little chuckle, Aaron stepped forward and wrapped his arms around her.

Melissa's heart pounded wildly. Why was he doing this? Hugging her as if they were old friends? As if he hadn't taken her virginity and then broken her heart.

"So we're paired off for the wedding," Aaron said as he broke the hug.

"So we are," Melissa said tersely. She was surprised that she'd found her voice. Her entire body was taut, her head light. She was mad at herself for having any reaction to this man.

"You're right, it's going to be a very interesting weekend indeed," Aaron said, echoing her earlier comment.

He looked good. More than good. He looked…delectable. Six feet two inches of pure Adonis, his body honed to perfection. Wide shoulders, a muscular chest and brawny arms fully visible in his short-sleeved dress shirt. His strong upper body tapered to a narrow waist. A wave of heat flowed through Melissa's veins, and she swallowed at the uncomfortable sensation. She quickly averted her eyes from his body and took a sip of champagne, trying to ignore the heat pulsing inside.

Good grief, what was wrong with her? She should be immune to Aaron's good looks. And yet she couldn't deny the visceral response that had shot through her body at seeing him again.

It was simply the reaction of a woman toward a man who was amazingly gorgeous. She wasn't dead, after all. She could find him physically attractive even if she despised him.

Although *despised* was too strong a word. He didn't matter to her enough for her to despise him.

Still, she couldn't help giving him another surreptitious once-over. He had filled out—everywhere. His arms were bigger, his shoulders wider, his legs more muscular. His lips were full and surrounded by a thin goatee—and good Lord, did they ever look kissable…

"I can't believe it's been ten years," Aaron said.

He didn't even remember. Why was she surprised? And worse, why was she irked?

"Closer to twelve," Melissa corrected him. "Eleven years, nine months. Something like that." She shrugged, hoping he didn't think that she had kept track of the exact date that they'd stopped talking.

"You're right," Aaron said, nodding. "It is almost twelve years. Wow, time flies."

"It sure does."

Melissa could hardly stand this. She glanced away, and relief flooded her when she saw her sister and Tasha. They were chatting with a group of guests about thirty feet away.

"You look good," Aaron said. "Amazing, actually."

His eyes roamed over her face, then her dress, and heat erupted inside her. Oh, how Melissa wished she could pretend the heat was simply anger, but it was more than that. She could see in Aaron's eyes that he thought she was beautiful, and her body was reacting to that reality.

Betraying her was more like it.

"It really is good to see you again."

Somehow, Melissa stopped herself from snorting. Was

it really nice, she wondered. If he was so happy to see her now, why had he cut off all communication with her years ago?

Melissa looked in Arlene's direction, and finally her sister saw her. Arlene's eyes lit up, and she waved.

Melissa waved back. Arlene was a lifeline at this moment, and Melissa took it. "Ah, there's my sister. I have to talk to her about something."

"Oh—"

"Later, Aaron," Melissa interjected, then strode off without giving him a chance to say another word.

She didn't dare look over her shoulder. Her heart was still pounding, a ridiculous reaction. So what if she'd seen Aaron Burke again? He didn't have the power to hurt her anymore. Her feelings for him had died years ago.

Was he watching her walk away?

Why did she care?

She *didn't*. But if any part of Aaron felt a measure of regret at cutting her out of his life, then good. She relished that thought.

He was happy to see her…as if! Why would he even say that? Was he trying to make nice after all these years, pretend that he'd never hurt her?

Well, if he thought there was a chance the two of them could ever be friends, he had another think coming.

Melissa inhaled deeply as she neared her sister. She was finally regaining her composure and her dignity. So what if Aaron was sexy? One of the sexiest men she'd ever laid eyes on, granted, but what did it matter when his character left so much to be desired?

She hoped he was happy with Ella, but she wasn't about to ask him about his wife. Nor was she about to spend any more time with him than was necessary. She didn't want him asking her about her life, and she didn't want to ask him about his. She would be paired with him for the wedding, deal with him as minimally as possible, and then go home to Jersey and forget all about him.

She had done it once. She would do it again.

Chapter 4

Ryan Burke clinked a fork against his champagne glass, effectively getting everyone's attention. Tasha stood beside him, a permanent smile on her beautiful face.

"Excuse me, everybody," Ryan said, looking around at the crowd of people. "Will you all please head into the tent and take your seats? Dinner is ready, so I hope you haven't indulged too heavily in the amazing hors d'oeuvres."

Ryan patted his stomach, as if to say he was guilty of exactly that. There were chuckles among the crowd.

"As you make your way into the tent," Ryan continued, "be aware there are names on the tables indicating where you're to be seated. We figured this way there'd be less confusion and less scrambling. It's buffet style, so please wait for your table to be called before heading into the line." He gestured toward the tent, indicating that everyone could proceed.

Melissa and Arlene wound their way into the tent with the rest of the guests. Melissa was already getting a bad feeling about the seating arrangements, and she crossed her arms over her torso as she glanced down at the first table to find her name.

"Oh, here we are," Arlene announced.

Melissa hurried to her sister's side. As she looked down at the names on the table, her stomach sank, her fear confirmed. Aaron Burke was seated to her left.

Oh, good God…

Not that she should be surprised, since they were paired off for the wedding. But still, this was too much for her to deal with.

When most of the guests were seated, Ryan and Tasha stood at the front of the tent. "We'll commence with the buffet line in a minute," Ryan said into a wireless microphone. "But Tasha and I would like to say a few words first. As you know, this is a welcome dinner for all of you who have come from far and near to be here with us for our special day."

Melissa glanced over her shoulder, saw Aaron entering the tent and quickly took her seat. As she did, she continued to survey the crowd. Where was Ella? As Aaron's wife, shouldn't she be here? Melissa would expect the woman to attend if for no other reason than to gloat. To show off to all those who had returned to town just how special she was because she had snagged a Burke brother.

Aaron and his father, Cyrus, were standing near the entrance of the tent chatting. An old classmate, Douglas Hanover, walked past them, heading in Melissa's direction. Before she knew what she was doing, Melissa was jumping to her feet and practically throwing herself into Douglas's path.

"Douglas?" she all but squealed. "Douglas Hanover!"

"Melissa?" His eyebrows raised as a question flashed in his eyes.

"Yes, it's me." She beamed at him. "Oh my goodness, it's been so long." She hugged him and noticed that he was stiff for a moment before hugging her back. "I see you on television all the time," she said as they pulled apart. "I always trust your forecasts."

"You watch me on the morning news?"

Douglas was employed by a network in New York City, and Melissa watched him every morning as she got ready for work. "Every day," she said. "I'm in Newark."

"Ah, okay."

She glanced beyond Douglas's shoulder at Aaron, trying to not make it obvious that she was looking at him. He was staring at her, watching her with curiosity. Even when she'd left him and joined her sister and Tasha, she'd noticed Aaron looking at her here and there.

"You always said you wanted to be a weatherman," Melissa said and grinned widely. Did she look idiotic? Or like a woman flirting with a potential new guy?

Aaron and his father were walking toward the front of the tent now—and heading right in her direction. "We should get together for coffee sometime," Melissa said to Douglas, speaking loudly enough for her voice to carry. "I get into the city quite a bit."

"That would be awesome," Douglas said. "Here, meet my wife." Douglas extended an arm, and a gorgeous woman Melissa had noticed heading in their direction sidled up next to him. "This is Diana. She's one of the producers of the morning show."

"Oh…" Melissa wanted to slink into her chair. Not because she cared that Douglas had a wife. She was happy for him. But because she had hoped to find someone—anyone—with whom she could flirt. There was something about the intense gaze Aaron had been leveling on her that had her distinctly uncomfortable. If she had someone else with whom she could spend some time, maybe he would throw his wandering eyes in someone else's direction.

"Very nice to meet you," Melissa said, shaking the woman's hand.

Diana's smile seemed forced, and Melissa couldn't blame her. To her, Melissa must have seemed like a threat. A woman determined to pounce on her husband.

"Lovely to meet you as well," Diana said, her voice professional and poised but lacking sincerity. "Sweetheart, we should go get our seats."

"Of course," Douglas said. "Melissa, we'll talk later."

No, they wouldn't. Melissa had already made a fool of herself. She felt bad for her pathetic display of flirtation, but seeing Aaron had gotten to her.

She glanced at her old flame again, saw that he was indeed looking at her even as he spoke to another guest. She quickly sat back down.

"What was that about?" Arlene asked, her gaze following Douglas.

"I just… I guess I reacted as a fan," Melissa lied. "I watch him on television every morning."

Arlene didn't look entirely convinced, but Melissa was saved from having to answer any more questions when Ryan began to speak again.

"Thank you, everyone, for taking your seats," Ryan said as the last of the stragglers found their tables. "And thank you all for being here. Isn't it a great day?"

People clapped, and some cheered.

"Tasha and I are glad that the sun is shining and that the forecast for the weekend is clear skies all around. I put in a special request to Douglas, and he delivered!"

There were chuckles among the crowd, and Douglas waved a hand.

"But more importantly," Ryan went on, "Tasha and I are happy that each and every one of you is able to join us for our special occasion. This wedding wouldn't be the same without you here. So we thank you so much for taking time out of your schedules to be a part of this."

"There's nowhere else we'd rather be," someone said, raising a wineglass.

There was a round of *hear hear*s, and people raised their glasses in turn.

Ryan smiled. "Many of you here are in the wedding party, and some of you are dear family and friends. All of you are important in our lives in some way. So this welcome dinner is as much about thanking you all for being here with us as it is a cause for celebration."

Aaron slipped into the seat beside Melissa. She twirled the stem of her wineglass, pretending she hadn't noticed.

"Some of you asked why we're not having the wedding

here," Ryan continued. "And this is certainly a stunning location. But aside from the fact that this house might not hold all the guests my wife-to-be wanted to invite…" Ryan glanced down at Tasha, who was now seated, and she gave him a sheepish smile. "It's also very important to Tasha and to me that we have our wedding in a church. We want God's blessing on our union, and we feel that's the right way to do it."

"Amen," Cynthia Burke said. Beside her, Cyrus patted her hand.

The one thing that Melissa had always liked about Cyrus and Cynthia was their absolute devotion to each other. Even as a child, she had seen how much they loved each other. How odd that their sons had become such players, despite the example of their loving and doting father.

Why was she even thinking about this?

But she knew why. She could feel the heat emanating from Aaron's body beside her, and it was stressing her out.

Tasha got to her feet and took the microphone from Ryan's hand. "But despite the number of people attending the wedding, it will still have an intimate feel. Because we love each and every one of you so much. Blood or not, you're all family."

Melissa lifted the bottle of Riesling that was on the table and poured some into her glass. A whiff of Aaron's cologne, musky and masculine, wafted into her nostrils. The heat from his body continued to radiate toward her, and she had to swallow.

He was entirely too much man. The problem was, he knew it.

She should be counting her lucky stars that their relationship had fallen apart. God forbid, what if they'd gotten married? He would've broken her heart the way he had Ella's.

Ella had fought so hard to snag a Burke brother, no doubt

for the bragging rights, but she'd had to endure Aaron's infidelity. Successful soccer player, wanted by many women around the world—it was no wonder that he had such an inflated sense of ego and had not been able to remain faithful.

At least Melissa had avoided that very life, a life she would not have been able to deal with. She didn't care how successful a man was; she demanded fidelity. She would not stand by her man as he cheated on her, just to keep the facade of a happy home and to maintain whatever luxuries she had become accustomed to. Material things didn't matter when your heart was breaking over and over again.

"Melissa, will you pass the wine?" Aaron asked.

A simple request, yet Melissa wanted to pretend she hadn't heard him. But a nanosecond later, she knew the evening would be that much harder if she played this game.

So she raised the bottle and poured him a glass.

Carlton appeared at the table then and took a seat on her right. She had already learned that he would be paired with her sister for the wedding.

"Melissa Conwell," Carlton said, smiling warmly at her. "It's good to see you again."

"It's good to see you as well," Melissa said, and she was glad that she had Carlton to chat with. It saved her from having to spend more time talking to Aaron.

"I can see that the staff is itching to take over," Ryan said, glancing at a man standing off to the side who was dressed like a butler. "But despite the table numbers, I'd like to ask that the table with my parents, grandparents and our gracious hosts for this evening, my uncle Cyrus and aunt Cynthia, make their way to food line first. Please, everyone, give them a round of applause."

People clapped as two generations of Burkes stood. They acknowledged the guests with warm smiles before making their way over to the food.

A hum of chatter filled the tent. Wilma, Tasha's aunt,

was seated with them because she was in the wedding party, and Melissa was glad that she was. Wilma was a talker, the type who liked to be the center of attention. She regaled the table with a story about how she'd been out with one of her sons in Buffalo and people thought they were dating. Wilma was in her fifties, but looked no older than her late thirties. She loved that no one was able to guess her age.

"So, Melissa," Aaron said.

She started to turn toward him, but the butler called their table then, announcing that they could proceed to get their food.

Melissa was the first one to jump up.

Anything to escape Aaron.

Chapter 5

She was ignoring him.

Aaron had made that determination shortly into dinner, when Melissa turned her attention to those on her right and kept it there throughout the night. She threw her head back and laughed many times, as though the conversation on that side of the table was utterly fascinating. She barely threw him a second glance as she proceeded to have the time of her life engaging with everyone at the table but him.

Which meant only one thing. She was angry with him. Maybe she even hated him.

Almost twelve years had passed since he'd last seen her, and apparently those years had not been long enough to bury any animosity between them. He had hoped that now, years later, with both of them more mature, they could rekindle their friendship. Even though things had fallen apart between them, he'd missed her friendship.

She had been a godsend in his life that summer when they'd dated, especially when he had been able to open up about the tragedy that had shaped his life. His little sister, Chantelle, had drowned. On his watch. He'd never been able to forgive himself.

Every great milestone he'd achieved had been marred by guilt. Good things were happening for him, yet Chantelle was dead. Did he actually deserve happiness when it was his fault that his sister had drowned?

That dark cloud had hung over him his whole life, even now, no matter how hard he'd tried to shake it.

That night he'd opened up to Melissa, she'd assured him that he did deserve love, happiness and success. And he had so wanted to believe her. Their relationship had seemed perfect, but perfect never lasted, did it? He'd learned that with Chantelle, so before it was too late, he'd ended the relationship with Melissa.

"Did you try the cheesecake?" Arlene asked, extending the plate of bite-size desserts past Carlton and toward Melissa. "This is to die for."

"No, let me try one."

Melissa took the plate of desserts, plucked a cherry cheesecake, then placed it beside the fruit on the small plate she already had. She didn't bother to extend the dessert plate to Aaron; she just put it down.

Aaron smirked slightly. Yeah, she was upset with him.

At the front of the tent, Ryan stood and spoke into the microphone. "Just so you all know, the party's not over. Please join us for some dancing. DJ, hit it!"

The next instant, a funky old school tune exploded from the speakers. People were standing, sitting or chatting, and some now made their way out of the tent, jiggling their bodies as they did.

"Please, enjoy the bar, the dance floor, the music," Ryan went on. "The dinner is over, but the night is young. And the wedding is in two days, so you can sleep in tomorrow."

Melissa quickly got up from the table and walked over to Arlene. They shared some conversation that Aaron couldn't hear. His eyes were on her, watching her every move.

She was mesmerizing. She was as enthralling as she had been when he'd known her years ago. If she had come here hoping to avoid him, she should have picked anything other than the sexy red dress she was wearing. Because she had his attention. And he couldn't keep his eyes off her. She was the most gorgeous woman here.

The dress was stunning. The formfitting, stretchy fabric highlighted her hourglass figure. She was the epitome of a sexy vixen, with those large breasts, narrow waist and voluminous hips. The black pumps she was wearing had a streak of red on the underside, and Aaron found himself thinking about sex.

With her.

As soon as he could get her naked.

Her hair was pulled up into a chignon and he wished more than anything that he could hold her in his arms, release the hairpins and let those raven strands down. He was tired of her frosty reaction to him, and he wanted to help her warm up to him and unleash her inner vixen.

The first song faded into another upbeat tune. "Ooh, that's my song!" Bonnie exclaimed. She took both Melissa and Arlene by the hand and pulled them out from the tent. The three women made their way to the dance floor that had been set up while everyone ate dinner. Aaron watched them go, his eyes fixed on the shapely figure in the red dress.

Out of nowhere, his brother Keith, younger by a year, appeared and plopped himself down on the chair that Melissa had vacated.

"Have you finalized the plans for the bachelor party?" Keith asked.

Aaron nodded. "The limo's arriving at eleven."

"And he knows nothing about it?"

"Ryan is clueless."

Keith smiled. "Good."

Melissa had had enough, and she kicked off her heels. She wiggled her bare toes, hoping to bring circulation back into them. The shoes were beautiful, one of her rare splurges, but she could only wear them for so long. She had passed the threshold of comfort quite some time ago. There was no way she could continue on the dance floor in these.

"Whoever invented high heels wanted to torture women," Melissa said above the music. She was dancing with Arlene now, as Bonnie had bopped off somewhere else.

"That's why I wear flats as much as I can," Arlene said, then raised a foot to show her sensible flat sandals.

Melissa typically did sensible, but today, she'd wanted to do something different. Wanted to come back to Sheridan Falls and make a certain someone realize what he'd missed out on. The beauty of it was, Aaron could only look but not touch, because he was married.

Speaking of married, where was his wife? She hadn't been here all evening.

Arlene leaned close and asked, "Are you going to the bachelorette party?"

"I'm here, so I guess I'm going to join everyone as we make the rounds."

"I'm not sure I'll be able to make it." Arlene frowned. "Craig says he's busy tonight, and he's giving me a hard time about being a neglectful mom. I might have to pick up Raven from the babysitter's."

"Neglectful mom? What the heck is he talking about? You're an awesome mother."

"He's just…he's finding any excuse to pick a fight with me. I don't know if I have it in me tonight to argue with him."

"How's he even going to know if you go out?" Melissa asked.

Arlene's lips twisted as she looked at her. "This is a small town, remember?"

Her sister was right. The smallest of news spread like wildfire in this town.

"He's been on my case about having the babysitter watch her too much. I don't know how he expects me to hold down a job…"

"Why don't you ask Mom and Dad to watch her?" Melissa suggested. "He can't complain about doting grandparents."

"They're always coming through for me. Sometimes

I feel guilty for leaning on them too much. I don't know. Tonight I might just stay home."

Melissa's eyebrows shot up as she looked into Arlene's eyes, trying to gauge her sister's mood. "Everything okay? Is there more going on than you're telling me?"

Arlene shrugged. "I'm just a little bit stressed. Working, being a single mom…it's not easy."

"All the more reason for you to come out with us tonight and enjoy yourself."

Melissa knew that the plan was to head to Buffalo and make the rounds at several bars. Tasha was ready for her big night, complete with an outfit that would let everyone know she was a single woman about to be married. The bridesmaids were going to treat her to her last big hurrah, so to speak. Perhaps there would be some flirting, but nothing outrageous. They weren't going to have strippers or anything like that. Just enjoy a great time bonding before Tasha's big day.

"I'll see," Arlene said with a shrug.

The music had changed from a hip-hop beat to something slow, and Melissa watched as Ryan pulled Tasha into his arms in the middle of the dance floor. A smile tugged at Melissa's lips. It was nice seeing her cousin so happy.

"Mind if I steal you?"

Melissa's spine stiffened. Certainly Aaron was *not* speaking to her.

Swallowing, Melissa glanced up and over her shoulder and saw that her ears had not been playing tricks on her. "Steal me for what?" she asked.

"To dance with you."

Was he out of his mind? "Arlene and I are discussing something."

"No, you go on," Arlene said. "Dance. I'll talk to you in a little bit."

"But…" Melissa's protest died in her throat when Arlene smiled at Aaron, then headed off the dance floor.

Melissa wanted to scream at her sister. Why would she encourage Aaron dancing with her? She knew how much he had hurt her years ago. Besides, he was a married man, so dancing to a slow tune with him was inappropriate.

Aaron stepped forward and slipped his arms around her waist. Melissa stood as still as a rock.

"I won't bite," Aaron said, trying to urge her body to sway to the music. Then he leveled a charming smile at her.

Melissa could almost imagine his unspoken words. *Unless you want me to…*

Oh, he thought he was smooth!

Because she knew it would look ridiculous to stand ramrod straight while Aaron tried to lead her in a dance, Melissa moved with him. But she eased her body backward as far as possible so that people watching them wouldn't get any crazy ideas. The last thing she needed was to come back to town and be embroiled in any sort of scandal.

"So," Aaron began, "we finally have a moment to talk."

Melissa said nothing.

"Are you still going to give me the silent treatment?"

Melissa made a face as she looked at him. "What are you talking about? We've talked all evening."

He raised his eyebrows and pursed his lips. "You've barely said anything to me."

"I don't know what you expect me to say. I haven't seen you in years."

"True." Aaron was silent for a moment as he turned with her, edging her ever closer against his body as he did. He leaned in and said softly, "It really is good to see you again. You look amazing."

Melissa glanced up at him. She felt a tingle of warmth as she saw the expression in his eyes, something that looked a lot like attraction.

He held her gaze for a long moment, and God help her, the warmth turned to a searing heat. Why was he looking at her as though he wanted to…

To kiss her?

No, she must be imagining things. Maybe he was just fascinated that he was seeing her again. Maybe there was even some level of regret on his part, knowing that he'd let a good woman go. She could only imagine what his life was like with Ella. Despite that Aaron was rumored to be a playboy, she couldn't imagine that Ella made his life easy.

But that had been his choice, hadn't it?

The reality that he'd rejected her hit her anew, killing any bit of physical attraction she was feeling.

When was this song going to end? She couldn't handle this anymore.

"It certainly looks as though life is treating you well," Aaron said.

"It is," Melissa said, exaggerating the excitement in her tone. "My life is amazing. I have no complaints."

"That's good to hear. I always wanted good things for you."

Melissa wanted to roll her eyes and tell him not to be patronizing. What, did he think she'd lived a boring and unhappy life because he hadn't been with her?

"You're single?"

"That doesn't mean I'm not happy."

Aaron looked at her askance. "I didn't say that."

No, he hadn't. Melissa was being far too sensitive. She inhaled deeply and told herself to calm down.

"I'm glad you're happy, that life is going well for you."

"Thank you." Though Melissa didn't want to be conversing with Aaron, she figured she ought to offer something to the conversation. "And you've been very successful. Soccer worked out well for you."

"It did, yes."

"Well, that's what you always wanted. Congratulations."

"Thanks." Aaron released her to take her by one hand and twirl her around. Then he pulled her close again. "You know, when I found out you were going to be in the wedding party, I asked Ryan to make sure we were paired up."

Melissa couldn't help gaping at him. "You did?"

"I figured it'd be fun."

Was he out of his mind? *Fun?* Was that what this was to Aaron? A game?

She didn't know what was going through his mind. Maybe he was flirting with her because he was one of those guys who wanted to feel that no woman could resist him.

The very fact that he was dancing with her like this was disrespectful to Ella.

Again, Melissa wondered where she was. How had the Ella she'd known in high school given up this opportunity to gloat on the arm of her husband?

Aaron splayed his fingers across her back, making her skin tingle. He pulled her close as the slow song came to an end, and for one insane moment, Melissa reveled in the feeling of her body pressed against his. She luxuriated in the heat that consumed her.

But only for a moment.

Because the next instant, she pushed herself backward, though he refused to release her.

"I think that's enough," she said, looking up into his eyes. Why did he keep looking at her with that smoky gaze, as though he wanted nothing more than to get naked with her?

"It's not nearly enough," Aaron replied.

Melissa glanced around uncomfortably, certain that she would see disapproving gazes everywhere. Instead, she saw Tasha looking at her with happy curiosity.

"Maybe this is just your…*way*," Melissa said distastefully, "but I'm not going to become a point of gossip for this town."

"We're dancing," Aaron said, and when Melissa tried to extricate herself from his grasp, he used the opportunity to twirl her around again.

Oh, he was infuriating!

Even though the tempo of the new song was upbeat and didn't lend itself to slow dancing, Aaron snaked a hand around her waist and pulled her against his body. Despite her irritation with him, a fresh wave of heat washed over Melissa. She looked up at him, aghast, and saw that the edges of his lips were curled in a grin. He thought this was funny!

"Aaron, that's enough," Melissa said, her voice firm. She knew what would happen tomorrow. Phones all across town would be ringing, people gleefully sharing the news that Melissa Conwell had been getting all cozy with Aaron Burke at the welcome dinner for the wedding.

Finally, Melissa wiggled her way out of Aaron's arms and glanced around, trying once again to ascertain just how much of a spectacle she'd become.

"What's the matter?" Aaron asked.

Melissa guffawed. "You're not serious."

"I'm dead serious. I was hoping you'd be happy to see me."

Melissa wanted to give him a piece of her mind, but instead she forced a neutral look onto her face. Leaning forward, she said in a low voice, "I know that you're used to women fawning all over you, but this isn't Europe, where no one cares. This is Sheridan Falls. Everyone here knows you're married."

Instead of looking even a little embarrassed for his unflattering behavior, Aaron chuckled.

"I can't believe you think this is funny. Consider your wife. And what people will say. By tomorrow, all seven thousand residents in this town will be talking about us and our disrespectful behavior on the dance floor."

"If you'll stop for a minute, I have something to tell you," Aaron said.

Melissa frowned. "Tell me what?"

"Ella and I are divorced."

Chapter 6

"What?" Melissa exclaimed, and she was glad that another upbeat tune had started to play, drowning out her voice to those within immediate earshot.

"We divorced a year and a half ago," Aaron explained.

Melissa knew she must look stupefied. "You and Ella are no longer married?"

"Actually, that's not true," Aaron said, and Melissa's heart pounded furiously. "We split a little over a year and a half ago," he went on, "but our divorce was finalized six weeks ago."

She stared at him, blinking but saying nothing. He was lying. He had to be. Melissa would have heard.

But why would he lie about that? In this town of seven thousand people, there was no way he could get away with saying something so untrue.

"I heard you guys were having problems, sure. But I also heard that you retired and returned to Sheridan Falls to work on your marriage."

"There was no saving our marriage when I retired last year," Aaron said, "but that was the spin on the story."

Melissa frowned. "If you got divorced, then why haven't I heard? It's not like anyone can keep a secret in this town."

"Ella and I kept this one," Aaron said. "I was tired of everything I did becoming fodder for the rumor mill, so I made a deliberate attempt to keep the news of the actual divorce very quiet. I didn't want the headache of the press salivating over every perceived sordid detail. For Ella's part, I don't think she was too keen on spreading the news either, especially after she got a lot of negative feedback for some of what she said about me to the press previously. So she agreed to keep things quiet. We went to another city, got it done. Only our families knew, and they were sworn to secrecy. This is my first official event as a divorced man, and as such, I've finally been letting people know."

"Wow," Melissa said, stunned. "I'm completely shocked. I'm sorry, by the way."

Aaron waved a dismissive hand. "Don't be sorry. It was a long time coming."

Aaron and Ella had split. Melissa's head was spinning. What exactly had happened? Who had ended things?

Maybe it had been Ella who'd ended the relationship, finally tired of Aaron's womanizing. Or had he grown bored of her?

She didn't care, so why was she even thinking about this?

"I'm sorry nonetheless," Melissa said. "I'm sure it wasn't easy."

"Thank you," Aaron said. "These things happen." He shrugged casually, as if it was no big deal.

And maybe for him it wasn't. The little she'd read about him in the tabloids indicated that fidelity was something he wasn't interested in. Maybe Ella had finally gotten smart and put her foot down.

Aaron narrowed his eyes as he regarded her. "Do you really think I'd be dancing with you like this if I were married?"

Melissa hesitated. She wanted to say no, but how could she? Celebrities were a different breed, and their behavior often left a lot to be desired.

"Don't celebrities live by their own code?" she countered.

"So that's a yes? Even with my parents here?"

"You're a grown man. They certainly can't stop you from doing what you like."

Aaron narrowed his eyes as he regarded her. She wasn't sure what he was thinking, but she could see his disappointment.

"I wouldn't bring dishonor to my parents, Melissa. I thought you would know that."

I know nothing about you was what she wanted to say. But when she saw Arlene whizzing toward her behind Aaron, her body sagged with relief. Thank God. She needed an excuse to escape Aaron and this uncomfortable conversation.

But as her sister neared her, Melissa's relief turned to concern. "Arlene, what's wrong?" she asked, seeing the stress on her sister's face.

"I need a ride."

"What is it?" Melissa asked.

"Aaron, I'm really sorry to interrupt you guys," Arlene said.

"No problem," Aaron told her.

Arlene took Melissa by the hand and led her away, throwing an apologetic glance over her shoulder at Aaron. "I'm sorry, Mel."

Melissa waved at her concern. "No, don't be sorry." In fact, she could thank her sister. Her interruption was perfect timing. "What's wrong?"

"I came here with Maxine, and I don't want to disturb her. She's having fun." She blew out a harried breath. "I need to leave."

"Why?"

"Raven is pitching a fit and I've got to go deal with her. The babysitter says she won't settle until she sees me. Who knew four-year-olds could wield such power?"

Melissa's worry abated. She'd feared something worse was going on. "She'll probably calm down in a little bit."

"She's been acting out since Craig and I split," Arlene explained. "She's having quite the tantrum, apparently. I'd really better go now. If we're going out later and I can get her down, I can have the babysitter stay with her for the night. I know this is inconvenient, but do you mind giving me a ride?"

Melissa threw a glance over her shoulder at Aaron, saw

that he was still looking at her. He probably wanted to pick up the conversation where they'd left off.

No, thank you.

Melissa faced her sister and gave her a reassuring smile. "No problem at all. Let's go."

"Thanks, sis. You can always come back."

"Naw, I'm good. Plus, I'll see the girls later tonight."

"Let me say goodbye to Tasha and Ryan and Cyrus and Cynthia," Arlene said.

Together they found Tasha and Ryan, then the Burkes and said their goodbyes.

"It was so lovely to see you again," Cynthia said, holding both of Melissa's hands. "It's nice to have you back in town."

"It's good to be back," Melissa said. She couldn't help wondering if there was something to Cynthia's smile and warmth. Had she jumped to conclusions seeing her and Aaron together?

"Okay, let's get out of here," Arlene said.

Melissa fell into step beside Arlene. Only once they were on the deck and away from the guests did Melissa ask, "Did you hear that Aaron and Ella divorced?"

Arlene's eyes grew wide. "They did?"

Melissa had asked the question in part to gauge her sister's response. Though she doubted Arlene would know and say nothing. Arlene genuinely hadn't heard. Aaron *had* managed to pull off the impossible—keep a secret in this town.

"He told me when we were dancing," Melissa explained.

"Oh my goodness! I knew they were separated, but Ella always told anyone who would listen that they were working on their marriage. Obviously, none of my friends heard or *someone* would have told me." Arlene paused. "Can I share the news?"

Melissa shot her sister a sideways glance. "You just can't wait to start making calls, can you?"

Arlene couldn't help smiling. "Well, this *is* big news."

"Aaron said they've finally started letting people know, just now, so it's not a secret."

"It's not surprising," Arlene said. "The stories of his cheating were rampant. I guess despite what Ella said, she finally had enough."

"I guess so."

Melissa led the way across the driveway and out to the street where her car was parked. Aaron clearly had a way with women. Not only was he gorgeous, he was charming. And successful. With his level of success came a certain amount of confidence. Of arrogance. Of expectation.

It was why he'd so easily put his arms around her and pulled her close on the dance floor, as if he expected that his mere presence would drive her crazy. She didn't want to know how many women he'd seduced with that easy smile and just the right touch.

Still, her body couldn't quite shake the hint of excitement his touch elicited.

Good grief, she was pathetic.

She pulled her keys from her purse and unlocked the door, then tried to shake off the memory of Aaron's arms around her waist. A memory that brought her back to twelve years ago. Twelve years ago on the lake, under a moonlit sky, tenderly kissing the young man she'd thought she would love forever.

Losing her virginity to him.

That was ancient history, a very long time ago.

Melissa would do well to remember that.

Chapter 7

"**I**'m getting married!" Tasha exclaimed to everyone on the street as the bridal party exited their third bar.

There was some hooting and cheering from passersby, and Tasha threw up her hands and gyrated her body. She'd had at least three or four shots and was clearly feeling no pain.

It was just after midnight, and the bridal party was making the rounds in Buffalo's downtown core. Arlene had begged off, deciding to stay home with her daughter, who had been fussing a little too much and wouldn't settle. Melissa had also tried to politely decline the evening's festivities, claiming that her long drive from New Jersey had left her tired, but Bonnie had insisted that Melissa attend.

"Tasha wants you there. She *needs* you," the maid of honor had stressed. "This night is about all of us bonding as much as it is about Tasha's last big night as a single woman. If everyone starts bailing, how's she supposed to feel?"

Melissa had gotten the point and agreed to go out. She didn't have a child to use as an excuse, after all, and figured that at least tonight she could truly unwind and relax.

Unlike during the welcome party, where she hadn't been able to fully enjoy herself with Aaron around.

The five of them walked into bar number four, Tasha leading the way. Heads turned, just as they had when they'd strutted into the first few bars and when they'd walked down the street. All it took was a glance to realize that their group was out for a bachelorette party. Tasha was decked out in a plastic crown and veil, the word *bride* written in sparkling silver glitter on the crown. Strings of cheap plastic beads, Mardi Gras style, hung around her neck.

Wilma, Tasha's aunt, walked right up to the bar and found a space between two people sitting on bar stools. No one could accuse her of being shy or lacking self-confidence. Despite being in her early fifties, she had as much energy and spunk as the thirtysomethings. She'd already had to fight off male admirers—which really seemed to please her.

Melissa and the rest of the bridal party gathered close behind Wilma. "Ah, a bachelorette party," the attractive bartender said, his eyes volleying from Wilma to the rest of them.

"Yes," Wilma said. "My niece is getting married."

"Niece?" The man's jaw nearly hit the bar. "You mean she's not your sister?"

Wilma blushed. Melissa got the feeling that if she weren't happily married, she would leave a string of broken hearts in her wake. She probably had in her youth.

"You're too kind," Wilma said. The man sitting on the bar stool to Wilma's left got up and walked away, and Wilma quickly took his seat. "We'd love a round of shooters. Flaming sambuca."

Melissa opened her mouth to protest, but then stopped when the rest of the bridal party began to hoot and holler in agreement. They were having fun, and she wasn't about to be the party pooper. Especially since they'd taken a limo to Buffalo for their night on the town, meaning they could all drink and not worry about driving. Wilma's idea.

Besides, she was enjoying the camaraderie that she never got much of these days. As the program director at the Turning Tides group home in Newark, her days and nights were often filled with emergencies, bad behavior, court dates and dealing with one crisis after another. But it had been a long time since she'd gone out, let her hair down and had some fun.

"Five flaming sambuca shots coming right up," the bartender said. "By the way, I like your shirts."

Tasha beamed. "Thank you." She had wanted everyone to wear T-shirts that announced their role in the wedding.

They were lavender, one of the wedding colors, and *bride*, *maid of honor* and *bridesmaid* were printed in a white cursive font on the corresponding shirts. There was no mistaking that they were celebrating an upcoming wedding. They all had feather boas slung around their necks, adding to the look.

Bonnie leaned in close to Wilma and said, "We can't spend too much time in here."

Wilma glanced at her watch. "We've got a bit of time."

"What's going on?" Melissa asked, picking up on the air of secrecy. Bonnie and Wilma had been sharing quiet conversation for the last half hour or so.

Wilma raised her eyebrows and smirked as she looked at Melissa. "Just a little surprise for Tasha."

Melissa regarded her with suspicion. "What kind of surprise?"

Wilma raised a finger to her lips and indicated for Melissa to be quiet.

Oh, goodness. Were male strippers a part of tonight's plans? Melissa had *not* signed up for that! The last thing she needed was someone snapping a photo of her in some sort of compromising position and putting it on social media. Sure, no one would likely know who she was, since all of her social media accounts were set to private, but still. She'd never liked the idea of half-naked men dancing in front of her. What was the point?

Tasha sidled up next to her. "Shocking news about Aaron. I can't believe he got divorced and no one knew."

Aaron's divorce had been the topic of conversation during their drive to Buffalo. The news had spread like wildfire.

"You think you two will hook up?" Tasha asked.

Melissa's eyes bulged. *"What?"*

Two more people vacated seats at the bar, and Tasha hoisted herself up onto the stool beside Wilma's. "I saw you and Aaron earlier. You both looked pretty cozy, like you were having a good time. At the time I wondered what he was thinking, but now that I know he's a free man..."

Melissa's face flamed. Then she chuckled uncomfortably. "Um, I have no clue what you're talking about."

"The two of you on the dance floor, getting up close and personal." Tasha wiggled her eyebrows.

"What are you talking about? We were certainly *not* getting up close and personal."

"You looked real comfortable to me," Tasha insisted.

"Comfortable is the last thing I was feeling," Melissa stressed.

"You could have fooled me," Wilma chimed in.

Melissa's head jerked toward her. "What?"

"See," Tasha said, "I wasn't the only one who noticed." Wilma reached beyond Melissa to high-five Tasha.

"You two are killing me," Melissa said. "A woman can't talk to a guy in our small town without it being scandalous?"

No one responded to her, because at that moment the bartender placed five shooter glasses on the bar in front of them and said, "Five flaming sambucas for the most attractive bridal party I've seen in ages."

His eyes held Wilma's for a long while before passing over the rest of them. Oh, he was a charmer.

And his charm was working. Wilma took a number of bills from her wallet—far more than were necessary. She was going to leave him a big tip.

"What's your name, sweetheart?" Wilma asked.

"Peter," he answered, then skillfully filled the glasses, which were set directly beside each other so that their rims were touching, with one long pour. Tasha watched wide-eyed, as though this was the most fascinating thing she'd ever seen. And when Peter then used a lighter to set each drink aflame, Tasha cheered and clapped, followed by the rest of the bridal party.

Except for Melissa. Though she was having fun, Tasha's

comment had her feeling a little…flustered. She hadn't looked cozy with Aaron, had she? How could she? She'd been the complete opposite of cozy.

"Come on," Bonnie said, pushing a drink in the direction of each woman. "Drink up, ladies."

This night was taking Melissa back to her college days, though she'd never been a wild partier even then.

Tasha lifted her drink and held it high. "To Melissa getting reacquainted with Aaron," she said in a singsong voice. "Who, I must say, is sexier than he's ever been."

The women all lifted their drinks and downed them, but Melissa didn't. She stared at each of the women in turn, her stomach filling with dread. "What are you guys talking about?"

"We all noticed it," Wilma said. "You and Aaron getting close…the way he was looking at you."

"How was he looking at me?" Melissa regretted asking the question the moment the words left her lips.

"Um, as though he'd like to get naked with you!" Bonnie answered and started chuckling. "I've never even met the man before today and I could see the lust in his eyes."

Melissa wished her sister were here to defend her. She would tell them all that they'd been imagining things.

"Quick, drink your shooter," Maxine told her.

Melissa threw her head back and drank. Warmth immediately spread across her face. But whether the heat was from the alcohol or her embarrassment, she couldn't be sure.

God, leave it to people in small towns to jump to conclusions. This was ridiculous.

"I haven't seen Aaron in nearly twelve years," Melissa said. "We danced. We talked. Is that what it takes to get people excited in Sheridan Falls?"

"Are you seeing anyone?" Bonnie asked. "Tasha tells me that you and Aaron dated the summer before college."

Melissa tried to suppress her frown. She didn't even know Bonnie, Tasha's best friend who lived in California with her. How had Tasha managed to fill her in on *her* life?

"I always thought they'd make it work," Tasha said, and her expression became wistful.

Melissa wondered when this evening had become about her. Wasn't it supposed to be about Tasha?

"You aren't seeing anyone, right?" Tasha asked, her eyes lighting up with hope.

"Not right now I'm not," she answered. "But what does that matt—"

"That's a start," Bonnie said. "You're single, and now so is Aaron. So there's nothing to stop you from reconnecting."

Why any of this was of interest to Bonnie, Melissa didn't know.

"I just want her to find love," Tasha said, and Melissa suspected it was the alcohol talking. "I want everyone to find love."

"Who's talking about love?" Wilma asked. "If I were fifteen years younger and single, I know what I'd be doing. Heck, if I were just single…it's a good thing I'm happy with George."

"Now that's what I'm talking about," Tasha said. She high-fived Wilma, then Bonnie.

Melissa frowned. What was this? Some sort of conspiracy?

"You all are crazy. Actually, you all are drunk," Melissa corrected herself. "I see a guy again after twelve years and you think that I'm going to what—get married?"

"Get naked," Wilma clarified, and chuckled.

Melissa felt hot again, and was desperate to change the subject. She turned to Maxine, Tasha's older sister, and the one who didn't seem quite as boisterous about her and Aaron.

"What about you, Maxine? Have you been dating since your divorce?"

Undeniable Attraction

"I kinda chased Carlton for a while," she said, speaking of Aaron's older brother, the oldest of the four Burke boys. "But I just made a fool of myself. I don't know about that guy—he seems to have eyes for no woman."

"You don't think he's gay?" Bonnie asked.

Melissa doubted it. News like that would have definitely gone through Sheridan Falls like wildfire.

"No," Maxine said. "I just think he's…moody. He seems to focus all his attention on running the inn. Plus, since his wife left and went back down to Arkansas, he's kinda been a recluse."

Melissa couldn't help thinking that this felt a lot like old times. Girls talking about the Burke brothers. Which one they liked. Which one they hoped to be fortunate enough to date.

It was pathetic.

She had been one of those pathetic girls, but her interest in Aaron had never been about landing a Burke brother. Yes, the Burkes had been the most talked-about bachelors in town back in the day, and apparently they still were. They came from a great family, were successful in their own right, and their sexy looks only added to their appeal.

Melissa's connection with Aaron had been forged from a mutual bond of friendship that grew over that summer twelve years ago when they'd worked together. In fact, at the start of the summer she had vowed to never date Aaron, or any other Burke brother, for that matter. But something about him had gotten to her, and he had touched her heart. His compassion for the kids they were counseling, his easy humor. And like a typical girl, she'd fallen. Hard.

Dammit, why couldn't she stop thinking about Aaron? This was stupid.

"Another round of shooters?" Maxine asked.

"Actually," Bonnie said, sneaking a glance at Wilma, "we should be going."

"Already?" Tasha asked. "I like this bar." She glanced around at the decor, which ran toward Mexican paintings and artifacts. "I feel like I'm in Cancún."

"It's nice, but we've got to get going," Bonnie said, and helped her down from the stool. "We've got a tight schedule to keep."

"Thank you, Peter," Wilma said, her voice low and flirtatious.

"You ladies don't do any serious damage now," he cautioned playfully.

"What fun would that be?" Wilma asked.

"I wonder what the guys are up to right now," Tasha said as Bonnie led her to the bar's exit.

"Don't you worry about the guys," Bonnie said. "Ryan's celebrating his last night of freedom, and so are you."

Melissa could only imagine what the guys were up to. Probably something raunchy. Naked women dancing all over them. Aaron was undoubtedly reveling in the experience.

It was ludicrous that anyone was even talking about there being any spark of attraction for her on his part. They'd dated—and he'd dumped her.

All Melissa knew was that she was older, wiser and not about to be flattered by a guy looking at her, even if his smoky eyes were the sexiest she'd ever seen.

And now that she knew that the bridal party was practically taking bets on when she would bed Aaron, she was all the more determined to give him the cold shoulder over the next couple of days. Let someone else become victim to his charms. Melissa was past that.

Chapter 8

"Why are we stopping?" Ryan asked.

Beside him, Aaron clamped a hand on his shoulder. "You'll see, cuz."

Ryan shot him a suspicious glance. "I thought we were heading to a bar in another part of town. Isn't that what you said when we got back on this bus?"

"Actually," Aaron began, "some guests will be joining the party."

Music was blaring in the party bus and the drinks were flowing. The party was in full swing.

"Hey…" Ryan frowned. "I specifically told you guys no strippers."

"Just sit back and relax," Jeremy, Ryan's older brother, said.

"Jeremy, I promised your wife we wouldn't do anything scandalous. Not to mention I promised Tasha."

Dave, Ryan's friend and best man, made his way to the front of the bus. The song playing on the speakers changed to an old favorite, and the seductive words "Do you mind if I stroke you up" blared through the limo.

"You all ready?" Dave asked.

The doors opened. A twirling feather boa was the first thing that appeared. Aaron looked at Ryan, who was shaking his head. "Come on, guys. You know this isn't what I wanted for tonight. I just wanted to hang with the guys."

"Ryan," Aaron said, "stop talking."

"Wait, what?" Ryan asked when the woman fully appeared. She strutted farther into the vehicle, heading toward Jeremy. "What is this?" Ryan asked.

"Your surprise," Aaron answered.

Then he heard, "This isn't our bus," and his breath stopped. That was Melissa's voice.

"Sure it is," Bonnie said.

"Are there strippers on this bus?" was the next question. "Because I didn't agree to—"

Bonnie yanked on a hand, pulling the protesting woman up the steps.

Melissa.

Aaron swallowed. Though he'd seen her earlier, as his gaze settled on her now, he felt a fresh stirring inside his body.

Her hair was down, hanging just past her shoulders. She'd curled it, and it looked amazing, with soft tendrils floating around the front of her face. Her eyes were narrowed, her confusion evident as she checked out the occupants of the party bus. Aaron's eyes went lower. Her purple shirt clung to her breasts, and the white jeans she was wearing were like a second skin.

Wow, those curves.

His breath caught in his chest. She was beautiful.

Wilma shimmied her way over to Jeremy, while Tasha appeared next. Her eyes lit up, and then she began to giggle. "Ryan?"

Maxine entered the bus last, and she too started to laugh. Then, as was the plan, all the women in the bridal party headed toward their respective partners and began to dance in front of them.

Everyone except Melissa.

Aaron made eye contact with her and raised his eyebrows, hoping she would catch his drift that she was to play along.

Ryan, looking awestruck, hurried to Tasha. He pulled her against him and started to dance. Then he faced his groomsmen. "You guys got me. I thought you had strippers entering the bus. I was about to kill you all."

Tasha looped her feather boa around Ryan's neck. "You're not disappointed, are you?"

"Absolutely not," Ryan told her. "I couldn't be happier."

As the two started to kiss, the other men started to dance in front of their respective partners. Melissa stood, staring awkwardly around.

Wow, so she wouldn't even be a sport and dance with him?

Aaron slow danced his way over to her. He saw the flash of panic in her eyes. Was she really that unhappy to be around him?

Or was she feeling something else?

She crossed her arms, her lips pulling into a tight line. She seemed completely unhappy.

Aaron knew that things hadn't ended in the best way between them, but they'd both been much younger at the time. He'd hoped that this wedding would give them a chance to reconnect.

He stopped in front of her, but kept his body moving to the beat of the music. "Come on, Melissa. Smile."

"I… I thought I was being lured onto a bus with male strippers."

"Are you disappointed?" Aaron asked.

"No. Of course not. Just…taken aback. I need a moment."

Aaron glanced around at everyone else on the bus. They were either dancing or pouring drinks. Having a good time.

"We decided to have a little fun with the bride and groom," Aaron explained. "Make them both think we'd ignored their wishes and had raunchy things and debauchery waiting for them."

"Cute," Melissa said, but the tone of her voice told him that she thought the stunt was anything but cute.

Wow, she was a tough cookie. Despite the happy partiers around them, she stood still, as if determined to be miserable.

That wouldn't do.

Aaron slipped an arm around her waist and pulled her close. "Come on, don't be a poor sport."

She glanced around, and seeing everyone else having a

good time, she began to sway to the music with all the enthusiasm of someone with a gun held to her head.

"There you go," Aaron said, smiling. "It's not killing you to dance with me, is it?"

She said nothing, but at least she didn't pull away from him. He tightened his grip on her, his breath catching as her soft breasts pressed against his chest. Man, she felt good, smelled good. And even with annoyance in her eyes, she looked irresistible.

"You don't have to hold me so tightly," Melissa said, squirming a little.

Oh, she was feisty. Aaron wondered how that attitude played out in the bedroom.

"You're not interested in getting to know me again?"

Instead of answering, she cut her eyes at him. She was trying hard, but Aaron felt something simmering beneath her outrage.

Passion.

She was fighting the obvious attraction between them. Aaron urged her closer. "You feel good."

"Aaron, please."

"Please what? Whatever you want, I'll do."

Her eyes widened in horror, but he caught the flash of a spark. There was heat in her horrified gaze.

Good. He needed to know that he wasn't the only one feeling the pull of attraction.

"I'm not asking you to...you know that's not..." She could hardly get her words out.

He swayed with her slowly, looking down into her eyes. She glanced back at him awkwardly, then around at the others. It was clear she didn't want to look into his eyes.

Was she afraid that her frosty exterior would melt?

"Hey," Aaron said softly.

She slowly lifted her gaze, a question in her eyes. Her

chest rose and fell with a heavy breath, and her lips parted slightly.

Heat zapped his groin. Damn, he wanted to kiss her.

Aaron didn't know what he'd expected when he'd seen her again, but he hadn't really been prepared for this reaction to her. He had hoped to reconnect and renew their friendship. But this visceral pull? This was more than he'd anticipated.

All he could think about was getting her naked.

"I'm not the same guy you knew before," Aaron told her, his voice low.

"I know," she said. "I've read the papers. Seen the news stories. You've led quite the life as a star."

Aaron frowned. "You can't believe everything you read in the paper."

She rolled her eyes. "I'm sure."

"What have you heard?" Aaron asked. Though he pretty much knew. Everything he'd done had been reported—and exaggerated—in the media. If he had coffee at a café in Rome with a female friend, the paparazzi wondered who the new "flame" in his life was. Heck, some of the stories had been downright lies.

The piercing sound of a whistle sounded on the bus. All eyes went to Bonnie, who stood at the front. "Sorry, y'all, but it's time to go. We have to get back to our respective partying."

"Nooo," Tasha protested, but Bonnie was already locking arms with her.

"What have you heard about me?" Aaron asked Melissa, hoping she would answer.

Instead, she pulled herself away from him. "We've got to go."

And not a moment too soon for her, Aaron surmised. She was no doubt happy for the chance to escape.

"We'll continue this conversation later," he said.

"No. We won't."

She angled her jaw, trying to look defiant. But Aaron could see that she was flustered.

He knew the feeling.

Seeing her again had shifted his world off its axis. Gone was the shy, somewhat awkward teenage girl he'd gotten to know that long-ago summer. She had blossomed into a radiant beauty. A sexy, mature woman.

One he wanted very much to get to know.

Chapter 9

"I've never forgotten you. Never forgotten our time together."

Aaron's voice was husky, and his fingers were warm as they traced her face. Melissa's lips parted on a sigh. She could look into his eyes all day, every day and not get bored. How was one man so darn sexy?

"You don't have to say that," Melissa whispered.

"I'm not saying anything I don't mean." Aaron angled her face upward, lowered those full sexy lips and softly captured hers. The kiss sent a jolt of electricity racing through her body, and delicious heat tingled through her veins.

"Baby…"

Melissa reached for his face. But all she felt was air.

Her eyes flew open, a sense of disorientation and panic instantly hitting her. For a moment, she was confused. One minute she had been with Aaron, his lips on hers. His hands gently touching her face. Now…

She was in her old bed in her parents' house.

She'd been dreaming.

About Aaron.

For a long moment, she lay there, her chest rising and falling with harried breaths. Hadn't it been bad enough that she'd had to see Aaron? Now she was dreaming about him?

She needed her head examined.

Melissa turned onto her side, and that's when she felt the first stab of pain in her temple. Good Lord, her head hurt.

Then she remembered. The night before. Making the rounds at different bars in Buffalo. Having one too many shots.

Suddenly, there was a noise, some sort of blaring. It took

a full couple of seconds for Melissa to realize that it was the alarm clock on her cell phone going off.

She rolled over in bed and fumbled for the phone on the night table. Another few seconds passed before she was successfully able to swipe the screen and stop the annoying noise.

Then she dropped backward on the pillow.

For the first time in years, she was hungover.

Worse, she was aroused.

"I'm never drinking again," she muttered, then got out of bed.

Melissa took a long, cool shower, but it still felt as though her brain were in a fog. The throbbing headache would not subside. No surprise there. She hadn't had that many drinks in a long time. At her age, she could no longer drink like a college student.

She wanted to regret the previous night, but the truth was, it had been fun. And just what Tasha needed. Her cousin had had an amazing time, and she was no longer worried about the wedding and things going wrong. The night on the town had been worth it just to see her cousin happy—even if at the end of the night Tasha had ended up weeping, talking about how much she missed Ryan and that she couldn't wait to see him and never leave him again.

Melissa couldn't help chuckling at the memory as she got into her car. It was nice to know that her cousin had found that special kind of love. From everything she knew about Ryan, he was a stand-up guy. Unlike his cousins, there had never been a hint of scandal about him. She felt confident that Tasha was going to marry a man who truly did love her and would always honor and respect her.

The bridal party was to meet at three in the afternoon for coffee and pastries. Melissa would need the largest coffee she could get, with at least a couple of espresso shots.

Hopefully the espresso would help fully sober her up—
and keep thoughts of Aaron from invading her brain.

All the women appeared to be in the same boat when
they arrived at the coffee shop—hungover and badly in
need of caffeine. Wilma wore dark shades that she didn't
take off. Unlike the night before, she was quiet. She downed
two cups of coffee in no time, but Melissa got the feeling
that she would have preferred to have it injected into her
arm.

Melissa would have preferred that, too.

But despite everyone's clear fatigue and recovery mode
from last night, there were some smiles and a definite sense
of satisfaction throughout the group.

"Does anyone know whatever happened to all the beads
I had?" Tasha asked.

"You started giving them away to random guys," Melissa said. "They gave you a kiss on the cheek, you gave
them a bead. It was all very…cute."

"Why do I have no memory of that?" Tasha asked.

"Because you had way too much to drink, my dear,"
Maxine said and patted her hand.

Only Arlene was completely fine today. "Sounds like I
missed quite the night. I could have used it."

"You can still let loose at the wedding. There are plenty
of good times left to be had," Maxine told her.

"I, for one, am not drinking again," Melissa said. "I'm
too old for this."

"Hush," Wilma said. "We've got a day to recover."

After enough coffee to keep them going and pastries to
fill their stomachs, the bridal party headed to the nail salon.
The salon owner had put out a big sign offering congratulations to Tasha in the back of the shop, and every seat that
was reserved for them had a string of flowers adorning the

sides and top. It was a nice touch, and the tears that welled in Tasha's eyes had them all collectively saying "aw."

Melissa gave Tasha a spontaneous hug. She was finally getting caught up in the excitement of the wedding. One more day, and her cousin would be married off.

Melissa wasn't excited about the rehearsal, however, which was to take place at seven o'clock at the church.

After last night on the bus with Aaron, Melissa felt even more awkward. Seeing him tonight and tomorrow at the wedding was going to be hard to endure.

Already, he was starting to invade her thoughts, and not in a good way. Why on earth had she dreamed of him? Imagining his lips on hers, his fingers softly skimming her skin… It was too much to handle.

She didn't know what it was about being back in this town and seeing Aaron again that had her so…flustered. It wasn't like her to even feel hot and bothered. She certainly hadn't spent restless nights dreaming of her last boyfriend.

As she watched the rest of the ladies settle into the chairs for their pedicures, it hit her just what was going on. Being away from work, her brain was unoccupied with the various crises she was used to and the day-to-day business of running the group home. Which meant she had all the time in the world to think about the here and now. And surely the alcohol didn't help—she was not used to drinking so much. Coupled with the fact that Aaron really was the sexiest man she'd ever laid eyes on, her subconscious brain could not stop her from thinking about sex.

Whoa…*sex*?

Though the women around her couldn't read her thoughts, Melissa shot nervous glances at them. She hoped that her eyes and facial expression didn't indicate what was going through her mind. She sat in the pedicure chair and tried to relax.

"I'm thinking of having one of my nails painted blue," Tasha said. "You know, for something blue."

Melissa tuned them out, her thoughts wandering back to Aaron. Was she really thinking about sex with him?

The zap of heat that hit her told her what she didn't want to accept.

Illogical, yes, given that she didn't even like him anymore. But she knew it was true.

Here she was, thirty years old and smart, and somehow Aaron's charm and good looks had gotten to her. The way he'd held her, moved his body against her when they were dancing, the scorching looks he'd leveled on her...

Melissa's brain and her libido were not in sync. Her brain knew that Aaron was bad news, but her libido...well, her libido had been turned on.

It's okay, she told herself. *Thinking about sex is fine. It just proves that you're still alive.*

And honestly, when it came to sex, she hadn't felt alive in years. Not even with her last boyfriend, Christopher. Her libido had come roaring back to life yesterday, and that was a good thing, wasn't it? She'd allowed an important part of her to essentially die.

Maybe when she got back to New Jersey, she would do what her best friend, Teresa—who was also the receptionist at the group home—constantly suggested: fill out an online dating profile and finally put herself out there. She did need some excitement in her life.

Two hours later, their nails and toes were done in lavender shellac, guaranteed to look perfect for the next day and beyond. From there, the women headed directly to the church.

"I'm sorry I didn't go out with you guys last night," Arlene said to Melissa when she got into the passenger seat beside her. Melissa had decided to leave her car in the salon's parking lot, and Arlene was driving them both to the church.

"You missed a fun time," Melissa told her.

"I could use some carefree fun. Craig has been driving me crazy. The thing is, I'm kind of worried that he's going to try to use anything I do against me. Like if I party too much, he'll say I'm an unfit mother."

Melissa's eyes narrowed as she looked at her sister. "Are you guys still fighting over custody? I thought you already won."

"He's not happy I was awarded primary custody. He does get Raven on the weekends, and I make lots of time for him to spend with her outside of that. But he still seems hell-bent on making my life miserable."

"Don't give him the power. You're doing everything you should be and more. You're a great mother. Don't let him drag you down."

"I'm still so hurt that he cheated. And he wasn't even original. He had an ongoing affair with his secretary." Arlene snorted. "She got pregnant—which is probably the only reason he told me about the affair. Then she lost her baby. I think he expected me to stay with him after that, and he's lashing out because I didn't. I mean, as if."

Melissa reached across the seat and patted her sister's shoulder. "I know it's tough, but just try to ignore Craig's rants and put-downs, whatever he's saying to you. It can only affect you if you let it."

"Honestly?" Arlene shot Melissa a quick gaze before returning her attention to the road. "My self-confidence has taken a beating."

"Come on, sis. Don't let him do that to you. That's exactly what he wants, by the way. Thank your lucky stars that you're free of him. There's someone out there who will appreciate you."

"I don't know. Maybe I should have just tried to make the best of things."

Melissa reeled backward. "You can't mean that. You know you did the right thing."

"Did I?" Arlene asked.

"Yes." Melissa squeezed her hand. "Never doubt that."

"But there are times when Raven asks me where her daddy is, and nothing I say seems to mollify her."

"But when she gets older and understands exactly what happened, she will know how strong you were. Your example that you shouldn't put up with anything just to stay in a relationship will be so important to her in the long run."

"But she's been acting out. There are times I worry that she's so unhappy, she'll be scarred for life."

"She's going through a period of adjustment. That's normal. But trust me when I tell you kids are resilient. Just show her constant love and she'll be fine. If the kids at my group home had constant love from their parents, they'd do so much better." Melissa paused. "Stop worrying. Everything will be fine."

Arlene sighed softly. "I hope so."

"I know so."

Arlene pulled into the church parking lot, and Melissa's pulse started to race. At least for a little while, she'd been able to put Aaron out of her mind.

But they were at the church now, and soon Melissa would be seeing Aaron again.

She wasn't looking forward to this.

Chapter 10

When the bridal party entered the church, the men were already there. Tasha speed walked down the aisle and straight into Ryan's arms. She hugged him tightly, as though it had been ten weeks since she had last seen him, rather than only half a day. Ryan dipped his head and kissed her softly on the lips.

"I missed you, baby," Tasha mewled.

Bonnie playfully rolled her eyes. "Girl, you've got the rest of your life to spend with him."

"Young love…so sickening," Wilma commented, then chuckled.

Maxine threw her a sidelong glance. "As if you're one to talk! You and George always out on date nights, holding hands and sneaking in kisses everywhere. You think word doesn't travel?"

"Of course I know it does," Wilma said. "I like to keep the gossips happy."

Maxine shook her head, but she was grinning.

"Hey, don't hate just because I keep the fire going," Wilma added, then snapped her fingers.

There were more chuckles, and Melissa quickly scanned the groomsmen. Aaron wasn't there.

Where was he?

And then she knew. The night had been young when the women had left the guys in their party bus, and who knew if they hadn't actually met up with strippers after that. And if not strippers, Aaron had likely met someone when they were out. A woman who was only too willing and eager to spend the night with him. He was gorgeous, and women no doubt threw themselves at him even if they didn't know of his celebrity status. Aaron was probably still exhausted and recovering from a night of pure carnal excitement.

No sooner had the thought entered her mind than the church doors at the back opened. Aaron breezed in, looking as though he had just stepped off the cover of a magazine. Dressed in a pale blue dress shirt that was open at the collar, Ray-Ban sunglasses and black pants, he looked drop-dead gorgeous.

He slid off the sunglasses and his grin illuminated the room. "Hey, sorry I'm late. Everyone been here long?"

"We just got here," Wilma told him, and Melissa noticed how the other woman's eyes lit up. Yeah, there was something about the Burke brothers that had women losing her minds. Even happily married women couldn't keep their eyes off them.

"Good, then I'm just in time," Aaron said.

He made his way down the aisle to the front of the church, and Melissa couldn't help noticing that even his walk exuded a sensual confidence. He looked good, and he knew it.

"How's your neighbor?" Ryan asked.

"She's better now," Aaron replied. "The doctors said that she has a mild concussion, but she's lucky she didn't fracture a hip."

"What happened?" Tasha asked.

"Aaron's neighbor, Mrs. Langley. You remember her. She taught fifth grade."

"Yes, of course," Tasha said.

"She fell this afternoon," Ryan explained. "And it's a good thing Aaron was there to help."

"Oh, no," Wilma said, her eyes narrowing with worry.

"Her house is across the street from mine, and I was walking to my car when I saw her heading down her front steps," Aaron said. "She went straight down, hitting her head on the concrete. I raced straight over to her, and she was nonresponsive. But she came around after about a minute or so. I didn't bother waiting on the ambulance. With the help of a couple of other neighbors, I got her into my car and took her to the hospital right away. That's where I'm coming from now."

"You're a hero," Bonnie said, smiling, and the rest of the wedding party shared their chorus of agreements. Some even slapped Aaron on the back, congratulating his efforts. Melissa stood rooted to the spot, a foul taste filling her mouth. It was the taste of shame. She had judged Aaron wrongly. She'd jumped to the conclusion that he had barely been able to tear himself away from some sexy vixen, while the truth was that he'd actually been helping out an elderly neighbor.

And Mrs. Langley, to boot. One of her favorite teachers in grade school.

"That is so sweet," Maxine said, laying a hand over her heart.

Aaron moved forward, heading straight toward Melissa. She realized then that she was the only one in the room who hadn't really acknowledged him. "Hi," she said, hating how breathless she sounded.

"Hi."

There seemed to be a glint in his eyes as he regarded her—or was she imagining things? "So, Mrs. Langley will be okay?"

"Yeah, thankfully. She'll have to take it easy for a while, but she's expected to fully recover."

"It's a good thing you were there, then," Melissa said.

"Sure was."

The rehearsal got underway. Even though they were just practicing for the big day, Tasha's eyes filled with tears nonetheless. It was obvious to anyone looking at her and Ryan that they had a real and special love.

Melissa's own eyes got misty as she watched Tasha walk down the aisle to join Ryan. She'd always hoped that by

this age, she would have found her own special man. A
man who would love her forever.

She glanced at Aaron. Saw him looking at her. He winked.

She quickly averted her gaze, but the heat that zapped
her body lingered, leaving her feeling flushed.

Sex with Aaron when he was a young man had been
amazing. What would it be like now that he was a full-
fledged adult?

Saturday morning dawned bright and beautiful. So that
all the ladies could be together and get up early to get ready
for the big day, Tasha had the bridal party staying at the
town's historic inn. The men were banned from going anywhere near its premises. Tasha didn't want to run the risk
of Ryan seeing her in her wedding dress before she walked
down the aisle.

"Something's wrong," Tasha uttered, looking around the
hotel suite with a panicked expression. She was dressed in
her off-the-shoulder mermaid-style gown, which was simply stunning. The bodice was decorated with shimmery
beads and pearls. So were portions of the bottom of the
gown that flared just above her ankles. Her makeup was
flawless, her hair elegantly put up in a chignon with soft
tendrils framing the sides of her face.

"You've got everything," Melissa told her. "Something
old, something new, something borrowed, something blue.
And you look…*wow*. I don't think there's ever been a more
beautiful bride. And I'm not just saying that."

Tasha worried her bottom lip. "No, something's not
right. I don't know what it is. I just… I feel it."

Bonnie went over to a drawer, opened it, withdrew a gift
box, then approached Tasha. "It's probably this," she said.

She extended the small white box, delicately wrapped
with a lavender bow, to Tasha. The box was attached to a
small envelope.

A look of surprise on her face, Tasha accepted it. "What is this?"

"A gift from Ryan. I told him I would give it to you when the time was right, and assured him I would know when that time was." Bonnie offered her a reassuring smile. "That time is now."

Opening her eyes wide, Tasha began to fan her face. "You give this to me now, after my makeup's done?"

"I'm still here to do any last-minute touches," Lizzie, the makeup artist, chimed in.

"Open it," Melissa urged, smiling. She'd been surprised earlier when a gift from Ryan *hadn't* arrived. Not that one was necessary, but she had figured that Ryan was the type who would send one.

Tasha took a seat on the sofa, and the women gathered around. She pulled the envelope off the small box, then opened it and withdrew a white card accented in gold.

"'For the love of my life,'" Tasha read, and her eyes filled with tears. "'My grandfather gave this to my grandmother on their wedding day, and now I'm giving it to you. All my love, Ryan.'"

Tasha set aside the card and quickly opened the box. And when she did, she gasped. "Oh my God."

"Let me see," Maxine said and angled her body behind Tasha's to get a better look.

In the box was a pair of teardrop earrings—one large diamond surrounded by tiny coral-colored diamonds.

"Oh my God," Bonnie said. "Those are gorgeous!"

Tasha was crying now. "I love Ryan so much. And now my makeup is ruined."

"Don't worry," Lizzie said. "I've got you."

"Help me get these earrings off. I have to wear Ryan's grandmother's."

Bonnie quickly got to work, removing the earrings

Tasha was currently wearing and replacing them with the ones from Ryan.

Tasha got up and walked to the mirror. When she saw her reflection, she beamed. "There. Now everything is just right." She glanced around at her bridal party before looking into the mirror once more. "This day is going to be perfect."

And it was. From the heartfelt personal vows Ryan and Tasha had written for each other, to the fact that there was hardly a dry eye in the church, the ceremony was deeply moving. Melissa had to hold back tears on several occasions.

More times than not, when Melissa looked in Aaron's direction, he was looking back at her. And even when he wasn't, she found herself checking him out. That long, lean body with its perfectly honed muscles. That chiseled jaw, those full lips. His smoky eyes that so easily lit her skin on fire.

He looked *good*. More than good. He was as hot as they came. Especially in that suit that fit his lean, athletic frame so well. Had any man looked sexier?

All the men were dressed in gray suits with lavender vests, ties and a flower to match the bridesmaids' dresses. The color combination was sharp and unique.

Ryan's suit also had tails, distinguishing him as the groom. He definitely looked handsome—but he had nothing on his taller, more athletic cousin.

Unlike the last two nights, Melissa wasn't freaking out every time her eyes connected with Aaron's today. The undeniable sizzle between them didn't send her into panic mode. She was past denying that she was attracted to him. The way her skin flushed when he locked his gaze with hers made their attraction incontestable.

In fact, somewhere along the line, she'd started liking the attention from him. Every time Aaron leveled his heated gaze on her, she felt a little thrill. She felt alive in a way she hadn't in ages.

Aaron was making her feel like a sexy, desirable woman. It was a nice feeling, and for now she was going with it.

"Are you still trying to pretend that you and Aaron aren't attracted to each other?" Wilma asked her when the bridal party followed the photographer onto the bridge overlooking a brook.

Melissa cast a sidelong glance at Wilma. Then she said in a hushed voice, "I never said I wasn't attracted to him."

Wilma's eyes grew wide. "Ooh! Okay, then."

Melissa chuckled. And wondered why she had just been so vocal about her attraction. Especially after spending the past two days denying it.

Maybe because she'd learned that Aaron was no longer married. Not that that changed how she felt about him in a romantic way, but something about his heated gazes and his seriously attractive physique was making her think about sex.

A *lot*.

Even at the garden when they were taking pictures, just a gentle touch from him on her arm or on the small of her back had her almost losing her mind. Her body was so ripe to be touched.

By Aaron.

Not until this weekend had she realized just how starved for affection her body was.

"Girl, he's single, you're single," Wilma said. "The two of you keep staring at each other like there's no one else in the world. I say go for it. I know I would."

Melissa glanced in Aaron's direction. As if sensing her gaze, he turned and looked at her. Then he smiled.

Such a simple smile, but it was breathtaking. The edges of his lips curled only slightly, but that was enough to light up his face. Lord, he was sexy.

And in that suit…he truly looked like he could be a model for a top Italian designer.

"Ladies on this side, men on this side," the photographer announced, helping arrange them alongside the bride and groom.

"This has to be the last picture," Betsy said. She was the wedding planner, and for the last half an hour she had been losing her mind. "We're already running twenty minutes behind, and we have to head to the reception hall. People are waiting. Let's get the show on the road."

The photographer ignored her and snapped off a few shots. "Groomsmen, stand behind your partners." When Betsy made a sound of derision, the photographer shot her an apologetic glance. "This is the last one, I swear."

The men and women rearranged themselves. Even before Aaron gently pressed his body behind hers, Melissa felt the heat. And when he placed his hands on her waist, her eyelids fluttered.

She swallowed, trying to center herself.

Every innocuous touch turned the heat up another notch—and they still had the reception to get through. How was Melissa going to handle another four or five hours being this close to Aaron?

The two of you keep staring at each other like there's no one else in the world. I say go for it. I know I would.

Chapter 11

Aaron wasn't sure when it happened, but at some point during the evening, he knew he would be spending the night with Melissa. She'd been giving him a certain look, playful and flirtatious, quite unlike the way she'd looked at him before today. Even her body language was signaling to him that she was interested. The way she would throw a glance over her shoulder, brush her finger against her lips. All subtle things that others wouldn't notice, but for him, the cues were loud and clear.

She wanted him as much as he wanted her.

That knowledge made it incredibly hard for him to get through the evening when all he wanted to do was sweep Melissa into his arms and out of the reception hall. But, of course, he would have to wait.

Somehow he'd made it through the hours of toasts and the dinner and the obligatory dances, his sole thought on when he and Melissa could ultimately get naked.

And finally, Aaron was seeing some light at the end of the tunnel. Tasha was about to throw her bouquet, then Ryan would throw the garter, and then he and Melissa could hightail it out of here.

"All single ladies to the dance floor," the DJ announced. "It's that time of the night!"

The single women obliged, most going willingly onto the dance floor, though some were dragged by friends.

"That's it, ladies! Who is the next one who will get married? It's time to find out!"

Aaron watched as Arlene had to pull Melissa onto the back edge of the dance floor.

The DJ began to play Beyoncé's "Single Ladies," and Tasha teased and tempted, raising the bouquet high, then lowering it a few times, causing the women to gently push each other, vying for position to catch the flowers.

Except for Melissa. She stood near the back, looking bored.

Finally, Tasha threw the bouquet. It went flying over the heads and hands of eager women and straight to Melissa. Aaron watched as her eyes widened in surprise. Then she did the only thing she could—she reflexively put her hands out and caught the bouquet, looking completely stunned that she now possessed the coveted floral arrangement.

People clapped and cheered, then Melissa forced a smile onto her face and took a bow.

"Okay, guys. You know what that means. It's your turn. Once Ryan accomplishes the task of removing the garter!"

Someone brought a chair onto the dance floor, and the DJ played a sexy tune. Tasha made her way onto the chair. Ryan stood several feet in front of her, grinning. As the music played, he did a sexy strut toward her, gyrating his hips. And when he bent onto his haunches and slipped his hands beneath Tasha's gown, some of the guys hooted and hollered.

"Get it, cuz!" Aaron's brother Keith yelled.

Ryan made the removal of the garter a seductive art, smoothing his palms up Tasha's legs and ultimately using his teeth to drag the garter down. The applause and cheers were raucous.

"Okay, where are the single guys?" the DJ asked. "Head onto the dance floor."

Aaron made his way onto the floor with his brothers and the other unattached men in attendance.

Ryan did the same thing Tasha had, teasing the eager guys by feigning that he was about to throw the garter a few times. And when he finally tossed the blue garter into the air, almost all of the guys leaped and tried to get it.

It was just about to land into the hands of another guy,

but Aaron jumped and stretched his body, much the way he would on the soccer field, and felt his fingers ensnare the silky fabric.

He emerged victorious, holding the garter high. He did a victory walk around the dance floor, the other groomsmen patting him on the back in congratulations.

"All right!" The DJ sounded excited. "Now, someone bring the chair back. Where's the lady who caught the bouquet?" The DJ found Melissa in the crowd and pointed. "Yes, you. Come take a seat on the chair."

Melissa's eyes widened in alarm. Bonnie and Wilma both gave her a gentle shove in the direction of the dance floor.

"And you." The DJ pointed at him. "You know what you're going to do, don't you?"

The DJ began to chuckle. And Aaron was getting a pretty good idea.

"That's right," the DJ went on. "You're going to put the garter *onto* her leg!"

Aaron shot a glance at Melissa, who looked like a deer caught in headlights. She had not been expecting this. Neither had he—but he couldn't deny the rush of excitement that shot through him at the prospect of smoothing his hands over Melissa's shapely legs.

Melissa looked mortified, while Wilma and Bonnie were already cheering. And when the DJ began to play R. Kelly's "Sex Me," the cheering became a frenzy.

The crowd wanted a show, and Aaron was going to give them one.

He moved his body to the beat, slowly approaching Melissa. God, the way her eyes widened as he neared her...he couldn't wait to be alone with her.

Aaron swiveled his hips slowly, in a motion meant to turn her on. Right now, he was her private dancer, the crowd be damned.

Melissa blushed, then covered her mouth. Aaron held her gaze and twirled the garter around on his finger. Then he gyrated his hips until he was lowered onto his haunches before her. He slipped his hands beneath her dress and lifted one leg. The crowd went wild.

And damn, his pulse went into overdrive. Her skin was bare and smooth, and just touching her like this was getting him aroused. He looked at her toes, painted lavender to match her dress, and he felt a zap of heat in his groin. He wanted her in nothing but these silver shoes later at his place.

Aaron met her eyes, and there was that look again. Beneath the hint of embarrassment that they were doing this in front of everyone, he saw an undeniable flash of longing.

He slipped the garter over her shoe and pulled it up to her ankle. Then he extended his hands, making them visible to everyone watching, and used his teeth to pull the garter up to her knee.

The groomsmen hooted. Someone whistled. Melissa's eyes grew as wide as saucers.

Easing his head back, Aaron offered her a smile. Then he used his hands to pull the garter just above her knee, keeping it rated PG. He winked at her. She continued to meet his gaze, and he didn't miss the way her sexy chest rose and fell with a heavy breath.

Aaron stood tall, raised his hands in triumph, then bowed as people applauded. Glancing in Melissa's direction, he saw that she was still seated on the chair. He knew she was frazzled, but he was betting that it was in a good way.

He walked back over to her and offered her his hand. She accepted it, and he helped her to her feet. But he didn't release her when once she was standing. Instead, he pulled her body against his and leaned his head to her ear.

"You're driving me crazy. What do you say we get out of here?"

* * *

Heat rushed through Melissa's body with Aaron's words. Her body was practically an inferno. After that erotic garter escapade, she was barely breathing.

Aaron touching her leg, using his teeth to pull the garter up it…that was more foreplay than Melissa had had in nearly two years.

She was driving *him* crazy? He was making her crazy with need.

Her attraction to him was fierce. Something she could no longer deny. She'd been fighting a losing battle since she'd arrived in town.

The battle to resist him.

"You're good at this, aren't you?" she asked.

"Good at what?"

"Good at being so darn irresistible," she admitted.

There. She'd said it. She couldn't deny it any longer, and she didn't want to. The truth was, she wanted Aaron. She wanted a taste of him again. Maybe then she could fully get him out of her system.

"You find me irresistible?" His eyes lighting up, he drew his bottom lip between his teeth, indicating to her that he knew just how enticing he was.

"You're good at making a woman weak with need," Melissa said softly. "Good at making her want you."

"Baby, you ain't seen nothing yet."

The words were a promise. A promise that Melissa wanted him to fulfill.

One night with Aaron…it wasn't something she'd ever imagined before she'd arrived in Sheridan Falls, but right now she wanted nothing more.

She would satisfy an itch that needed to be scratched, then go her merry way.

"I can only imagine," Melissa said softly.

Aaron splayed his hands over her back and urged her

against him. Then he looked into her eyes for a long moment, and it felt as though they were the only two people in the room. "You don't have to imagine," he said.

Melissa glanced around, wondering if prying eyes were checking out their interaction. "You really want me to leave with you?"

"Am I in some way being unclear?"

He whispered the words in her ear, and Melissa's body shuddered. No, he wasn't being unclear. Not at all.

But she was hesitating. Was she really contemplating spending the night with Aaron?

Heck yes, she was. One night of carnal bliss...she needed it.

"What do you say?" Aaron whispered, and Melissa's eyelids fluttered shut.

She gripped his shoulders, needing to hold on to him before she swayed on her feet. He was having that much of an effect on her. Looking into his eyes, she said, "I don't want the night to end."

Aaron's lips curled in a slow, satisfied grin. "Good. Because I don't want it to end, either. I'm just trying to figure out the right moment to get out of here."

He pulled her closer and edged his face lower. But he seemed to catch himself and remember that the roomful of wedding guests surrounded them. So instead of kissing her, he whispered into her ear, "I haven't been able to get you out of my mind since I first saw you again. You've been occupying my thoughts at night, during the day. Hell, even when you left the room, I couldn't stop thinking about you."

Melissa's face flamed. It was silly, but his words stoked her inner fire. The idea that he desired her to that degree was a huge turn-on.

So what would it hurt? One night with Aaron, and she could get whatever this was out of her system and head back to New Jersey and her life.

"Why don't you get your stuff and head out of the hall as if you're heading to the restroom? I actually brought my car here earlier, so it's out back. I'll meet you outside in about five minutes?"

A few minutes later, Melissa put the plan into action. She didn't bother to say goodbye to anyone, not wanting anyone to be the wiser. Eventually they would wonder where she and Aaron were, but she was certain that no one would be concerned.

Melissa waited at the side of the building, and when Aaron rounded the corner toward the parking lot, she smiled. God help her, he was gorgeous. Every time she laid eyes on him, he took her breath away.

He returned her smile. "You wait here. I'll go get my car."

"Did anyone seem suspicious?"

"I left them going crazy on the dance floor. I don't think anyone noticed me slip out."

Maybe not yet. But they would notice soon enough. Though, honestly, she didn't care. Even if there were witnesses from the local paper who would make their tryst front-page news tomorrow, she was going to spend the night with Aaron.

She watched Aaron walk toward the back of the parking lot, his strong and confident gait turning her on even more. She could only imagine how skilled a lover he was now.

Well, she wouldn't have to imagine much longer, would she?

She was about to get it on with Aaron.

And she wasn't going to regret it.

Chapter 12

A little more than ten minutes later, Aaron was pulling his Mercedes sedan into a long, semicircular driveway. Sprawling trees blocked much of the view of the front of the house, and in the darkness you couldn't see much of it anyway. Melissa could see that the house was a dark color, likely red brick, with a large wraparound porch. It was big, with a spacious front yard, the kind of house that Melissa could imagine being filled with kids.

Aaron stopped the car and put it into Park, and Melissa inhaled a deep breath. She wanted to do this, was excited about doing it, yet her stomach flitted from nerves. It hit her full force that she was actually about to spend the night with Aaron.

There was no turning back now.

And she didn't want to turn back. Honestly, she hadn't wanted anything as much as she wanted this in a long time.

Aaron exited the car and hurried around to the passenger-side door. He opened it for Melissa, then offered her his hand.

She exited the car, then hugged her torso as she glanced around at the property.

Aaron placed his hands on her shoulders, then rubbed them down her arms. "Are you cold?"

"No. Just taking it all in." She turned to face him. "I like your place. It's serene. Not at all what I expected."

"What did you expect?" Aaron asked.

"Honestly? I guess I figured you'd have a place bigger than your parents', somewhere everyone can see it."

"I'm much more into my privacy, especially these days."

Melissa took a step toward the house, then abruptly stopped. "Wait," she asked, turning to face him. "Did you live here with Ella?"

"No. The big house you mentioned—Ella has it. I moved

here after we split." He put a hand on the small of her back. "But I definitely do not want to talk about Ella."

Melissa glanced over her shoulder at Aaron. "Neither do I."

Keeping his hand on her back, Aaron guided her toward the house. It was dark, but strategically placed lights on the porch provided soft illumination.

Aaron removed his hand from her body only to unlock and open the door. Then he took her by the hand and led her into his home. He flicked on the light switch, and the foyer came into view. A mahogany-and-oak table holding a statue of a horse was to the left beside the wall. An abstract painting hung on the wall above it. The staircase was to the immediate right and curved as it went up to the second level. At the top of the staircase was a lookout to the lower level. A massive chandelier with hundreds of coin-size crystals hung from the high ceiling and looked dazzling as the light played off it.

"Your place is beautiful," Melissa said.

Aaron drew her into his arms. "Thanks. Now can we stop talking and do what we've both wanted to do all day?"

He pulled her into his arms, and within a nanosecond, his lips were coming down on hers. Melissa expected fast and furious, especially with the buildup of the sexual tension between them. But instead, the kiss was soft and slow.

Heat unfurled inside her just as slowly.

Aaron's mouth worked over hers gently as his thumb stroked her jawline. His other hand moved to the back of her neck, his fingers tenderly touching her skin. Then they went higher, into the tendrils at the nape of her neck. It didn't take long for Melissa to realize that he was searching for the pins that held her hair up. Deepening the kiss, he maneuvered her hair free. Melissa could hear the soft pinging sounds of the hairpins falling onto the floor.

Her chignon successfully loosened, Aaron groaned and

slipped both hands into her hair. He swept his tongue into her mouth and tangled it with hers. A rush of excitement shot through Melissa's body. She crept her hands up his strong biceps and then wrapped them around his neck and held on as her head grew light from the most incredible sensations.

"This is what I've been thinking about all day," Aaron murmured. "And not just all day. I've been thinking about this since I first saw you again."

"You have?" Melissa asked.

"Yeah." Staring into her eyes, he pulled his bottom lip between his teeth and covered one of her breasts with his palm. "I've been going crazy thinking about you."

Melissa exhaled a shuddery breath. His attraction to her was like an aphrodisiac.

He kissed her again, his mouth moving hungrily over hers. And then he scooped her into his arms.

Melissa let out a little squeal, then giggled as Aaron rushed up the staircase with her. He headed straight down the dimly lit hallway and through an open door. The fact that he couldn't wait to get her to bed was turning her on even more.

Melissa expected Aaron to quickly put her on the mattress, but instead he stood at the bed's edge with her. He brought his mouth down on hers once more. Suckling softly, nibbling gently, he lowered her until she was standing. And then he continued to kiss her senseless. The sensations tingling through her body were heady and exciting.

He broke the kiss and whispered, "As much as I want to rip this dress off you, I know I shouldn't. Tell me how to get it off so I don't ruin it."

"There's a zipper at the back," Melissa told him, surprised at the sound of her ragged breathing. Her body was on fire. And Aaron hadn't even touched her in the places she craved the most.

He turned her in his arms so that her back was facing him, and he found the zipper and dragged it down. Slowly. As if his entire goal was to draw out the teasing to make her even weaker with need.

Once the zipper was down, Aaron pushed the fabric over the one shoulder and down her arm. His fingers skimming her skin were like tendrils of electrical wire touching her, zapping her with jolts of lust. She was loving every second of this.

Melissa shimmied her body, helping him to remove the dress. He guided it over her hips, and the silky fabric fell to the ground around her feet.

Melissa stepped out of the dress, then turned to face him. As he regarded her, his eyes slowly widened and filled with heat. She was standing there in her strapless bra and thong, and she'd never felt sexier.

Aaron's exhalation of breath was audible. "Damn."

He reached for her hand, then pulled her forward. She landed against his hard body with a little *oomph*.

His clothes rubbed against her bare skin. She wanted him out of them.

"Come here," he rasped. And then his mouth was on hers again. As his tongue flicked hungrily over hers, Melissa slipped her hands beneath his jacket and began to push the fabric off his shoulders. He helped her, shrugging out of it, his lips still locked with hers. He let the jacket fall onto the ground. Melissa then felt for the buttons on the vest and began to undo them one by one. He continued to kiss her, holding her face in his hands as he did, and oh, God, the feelings that were raging through her. They were intense and delicious.

Though her fingers and body were getting weak from the assault of his lips on hers, Melissa found the buttons of his shirt and fumbled to undo them. Finally reaching the last one, she pulled the dress shirt out of his pants. Aaron broke the kiss and hastily got out of the shirt and vest, as though those items of clothing were on fire. He tossed them onto the hardwood floor.

As Aaron undid the belt on his dress pants, Melissa reached behind her back to undo her bra. "No," Aaron quickly said. "Let me. I need to take off your clothes."

Need... Had more seductive words ever been uttered?

She licked her bottom lip as she watched Aaron finish undoing his dress pants then kick them off. Standing before her in only black boxer briefs, he stepped toward her. He slipped his arms around her body, found the clasp of the bra and released it. He slipped it off her, then tossed it onto the floor. Melissa's breasts spilled free.

Taking a step backward, Aaron looked at her. His eyes did a slow once-over, taking in every inch of her. "Wow."

"You look pretty incredibly yourself," she said, practically breathless from the raging desire flowing through her.

Aaron moved forward and pulled her against him with force. He captured her mouth in a ferocious kiss. He put his whole body into it, his arms wrapping tightly around her, his groin pressing against her belly. Melissa gripped his shoulders and hung on as her legs turned to jelly. Good God, how could she be so completely attracted to this man?

Making a carnal sound, he lifted her, and she threw her legs around his hips and secured them at the ankles. He moved with speed to the bed, and leaning forward, he lowered her onto it. Melissa's back hit the soft mattress. Aaron's body was still on top of hers as she clung to him, and she reveled in the feel of his smooth skin and hard muscles.

He slowed down the tempo of the kiss and softly suckled her bottom lip. Melissa sighed against his lips. Her body was alive with sensation, and it was amazing.

Aaron slipped a hand between them, covered her breast, then tweaked her nipple. They both groaned in satisfaction at the same time. Then Aaron broke the kiss and brought his head to her breast, flicking his tongue over her nipple. Melissa cried out as it hardened.

"Yes, baby," Aaron said softly.

Then he covered her nipple with his mouth and suckled softly. Melissa's center throbbed. "Aaron…"

He tweaked her other nipple to a hardened peak while continuing to suck the other one softly. He gently grazed it with his teeth, and Melissa thought she would lose her mind. She arched her back as a moan escaped her lips.

Aaron smoothed a hand down her belly and into her panties. He was gentle as his fingers explored, found her nub. He stroked her in a slow, circular motion, and Melissa thought her body would explode. That's how good this felt.

"I need to taste you," Aaron whispered.

And then he was moving down her body, positioning himself above her hips. He pulled her thong down. Melissa bent one leg at the knee to aid him in getting the underwear off. He slipped it over one of her heels, then the other, then discarded it behind him.

"Oh, yeah," Aaron said, his lips curling in a smile. "Do you know how sexy you are? Naked on my bed, except for those hot shoes?"

As Melissa held his heated gaze, she felt like the most desirable woman in the world.

Aaron slipped a hand between her thighs and stroked her, and she exhaled a slow, lust-filled moan. Then he lowered his head, his tongue gently flicking over her most private spot. Melissa gripped the bedsheet in her fists and arched her back. The feel of his tongue on her most sensitive spot was thrilling her beyond anything she had ever known.

He added his fingers, driving her even wilder with pleasure. Her breathing became faster, sharper. The pressure inside her was building. Taking her to the edge…

A soft flick of his tongue, then a little suckle, and Melissa was letting go. Falling into the sweet abyss of delirious sensations. Aaron linked his fingers with hers as she rode the delicious wave.

Then he got up, kicked off his boxers and went to his bedside table. Melissa's body was so spent from her earth-shattering release, she barely registered that he was getting a condom.

Aaron rejoined her on the bed, easing her legs apart and settling between her thighs. Then he guided his shaft inside her, slowly. Inch by delicious inch, he filled her. Melissa cried out unabashedly. "Oh, Aaron..."

"Yes, baby." He kissed her softly, then brushed his lips across her cheek. He kept going until he reached her ear. He drew her earlobe into his mouth and sucked on it tenderly. And oh, the sensation! That, coupled with the feeling of his shaft deep inside her, was raising her pleasure level to a fever pitch.

Aaron picked up the pace. His thrusts were harder, faster. Melissa moved her hips against him, matching his rhythm. She ran her fingers up and down his back, and he thrust harder.

Her release caught her by surprise. It came swiftly, starting in her center and tingling through her entire body. She dug her nails into his back, and Aaron's strokes became bionic. He was breathing heavily, his thrusts a steady, fast pace. Within moments, he was exhaling a primal cry. His body tensed as he succumbed to his own release.

"Yes," Melissa murmured, stroking his back tenderly now. She nuzzled her nose against his jaw as he enjoyed the full pleasure of his orgasm.

Several moments later, the weight of Aaron's body came down on hers. His heavy breathing mingled with hers, the only sounds in the room. Melissa curled a leg around his slick body, wishing she could stay there with him like that forever.

Aaron had just given her a sexual experience she would not soon forget.

Chapter 13

Melissa's eyes popped open. Sun was spilling into the room—a room she didn't recognize—through sheer curtains. She tried to move and realized there was an arm draped over her waist. It didn't take more than a nanosecond for her to remember.

She was in Aaron's bed. She'd spent the night with him. And he had rocked her world.

A slow smile spread on her face. They'd made love three times, each subsequent session lasting longer. Melissa had barely gotten any sleep, but she wasn't complaining.

She felt amazing. One thing was clear. She'd needed that. She'd needed hot sex, more than she had realized.

The last couple of years without any action had left her desperate for a man's touch.

She stretched her body to see the time on the bedside clock. Aaron groaned and held onto her tighter.

Melissa swallowed. He wasn't even fully awake, yet he didn't want to let her go. It felt nice.

More than nice. Aaron had been completely into her, and in his arms, Melissa had truly felt like she was the only woman in the world. The only woman he wanted.

But now it was morning, and the fantasy of last night had come to an end. She'd gotten what she wanted. One night with Aaron. One night that could keep her warm until her next sexual encounter.

She strained her body against Aaron's arm, and saw that the clock read 8:34 a.m. "Eight thirty!" she exclaimed.

Her outburst startled Aaron, and releasing her, he rolled onto his back. She glanced at him, saw his sleepy eyes and confused expression.

"I'm sorry," she said. "I didn't mean to wake you."

Aaron rubbed his eyes. "It's okay."

"I have to go," Melissa went on. "I didn't plan to stay here that long."

"Why do you have to leave?" Aaron asked. His voice was groggy.

"I have to get back to my parents'." She frowned. "I should have returned before they woke up."

"What are they going to do, ground you for staying out all night?" Aaron asked, smiling at her.

"No. I just…well, I don't really want them asking me any questions about where I was."

"Just say you stayed at Arlene's."

"Good idea," Melissa said, that thought not having occurred to her. She was entirely too paranoid about anyone knowing where she'd spent the night and exactly what she'd been doing.

"Or you can tell them that you had your wicked way with me," Aaron said, then laughed.

Exactly what she *didn't* want. "Um, sure. That'll go over well."

Aaron eased his body forward and snaked a hand around her waist. "Since you can use your sister in order to not get grounded, why don't you stay in bed with me?" He held her gaze, then bit down on his bottom lip. "I'm not through with you yet."

Melissa's woman parts tightened. Giving him a coy smile, she stretched her body out beside his. "Now that's an offer I can't refuse."

The sounds of someone moving around in his room caused Aaron to come fully awake. He opened his eyes and saw that Melissa was standing near the foot of the bed, slipping into her dress.

"Where are you going?" he asked.

"I really do have to leave," she told him.

"I was hoping we could maybe go out for breakfast."

When she threw him a glance over her bare shoulder, he realized that she would never be able to go out for something to eat in that dress. "Or eat here. My fridge is stocked. And I'm a pretty good cook."

Melissa tried to zip up the back of her dress. "Sorry, I can't. I have some things to do."

"All right. Can I see you later, then?"

"I have a dinner with the bridesmaids."

"Oh, that's right. The thank-you dinners." Aaron had forgotten about the dinner he was supposed to attend with the groomsmen. Ryan and Tasha wanted to spend a bit of time with their wedding party before they headed off on their honeymoon. Aaron wished they'd opted for one dinner with the men and women, but Ryan and Tasha were having separate dinners.

"I'm game to see you after that…" Aaron suggested.

Melissa's lips curled in a smile. "I'll check my schedule. See if I'm available."

Aaron chuckled softly. "When will you let me know if your schedule is clear?"

She headed toward the bed. "Will you zip me up?"

"Sure." Aaron maneuvered himself to a sitting position, then zipped up the dress. "There you go."

"Thanks."

"Seriously, I'd like to see you again," he said. "Maybe we can go for a drink after dinner?"

"We'll just have to see, won't we?"

Oh, so she was going to be like that. Make him work for it.

"Let me get up. I'll take you to your parents'."

"There's no need. I already called a taxi. It's on the way."

Aaron frowned. "Oh. So no time for coffee?"

"No time." Melissa sat on the bed beside him, her eyes lighting up playfully. "Thank you for the night, sir."

"I hope we'll have another one."

"If I'm in town, sure," she said flippantly.

"What do you mean by that?"

"I may be heading back to New Jersey before you get the chance to see me again."

Aaron cast her a sidelong glance. She was playing with him. Making him work for it, as he suspected. "I definitely plan to see you before you leave. I'm going to need to." She gave him a little smile, then got up and collected her shoes.

"Give me your number. It'll make getting in touch with you much easier."

"You know where to find me…if you want to."

"You're really not going to give me your number?"

"This is a small town. I won't be hard to find."

Then Melissa took a few steps toward the bedroom door. Was she really going to leave like this?

She seemed to think better of it and turned around. She made her way back to the bed and gave him a soft kiss on the lips. "Really, I had a great time," she said huskily. "Thank you for last night."

"You're welcome."

Aaron wanted to wrap an arm around her and hold on tight so she couldn't leave.

But he would see her again. There was no doubt about that.

Aaron decided not to rush the chase. He'd give Melissa enough time to miss him. Though as the next morning rolled around, he wished that he could have seen her last night after the dinner with the groomsmen. His thoughts had been on her the entire time.

Aaron hoped that as Melissa had been enjoying drinks and dinner with the bridesmaids, she was also remembering her night with him. Because that's what he had been doing. Remembering every fantastic moment of their night together. The way she'd felt in his arms. The way she'd kissed him so eagerly. The first moment he'd gotten to see her amazing body without clothes on.

Even Ryan had commented that Aaron didn't seem "fully there" last night, which was true. He had been with the guys physically, but mentally, he'd been in his bedroom with Melissa, making her sigh and moan.

He was eager for round two.

She had to want the same thing, given the electricity between them in the bedroom.

Aaron rolled over in his bed and sat up. Time to stop thinking about Melissa and find her. They'd both had a night to miss each other, and that had been enough for him.

He got up, showered and dressed, then headed to one of the local cafés for coffee and a bagel. Afterward, he went next door to the flower shop, where he picked up a small bouquet. Nothing over-the-top, but enough to let Melissa know that he liked her. He hoped that she would agree to spend the day with him. Maybe they could head into Buffalo for lunch, follow up with a movie. Then they could head back to his place.

Aaron pulled up to the Conwell residence and parked on the street. He was well acquainted with the Conwells, not only from having grown up in this small community, but because of the summer when he dated Melissa. He'd dropped by often then to pick her up for work or to bring her home.

He exited his car, grabbed the bouquet, then made his way to the front door. He rang the doorbell.

Less than a minute later, Melissa's mother, Valerie Conwell, answered the door.

"Why, hello, Aaron." Valerie's lips spread into a bright smile. "It's so nice to see you."

"Very nice to see you as well, Mrs. Conwell," Aaron said.

"And you brought flowers." Her eyes twinkled. "They're

lovely. Would you like to come in for a moment? I've got some tea and freshly baked biscuits."

"That sounds lovely," Aaron said, just as the smell of the biscuits wafted into the room. "But I've already eaten. I was just wondering if Melissa is here."

"Oh." Valerie's face twisted in confusion. She glanced at the flowers, seeming to fully understand now. "Aaron, she left. She headed back to New Jersey this morning."

Aaron stared blankly at Valerie, unsure he understood what she'd just said. In fact, he was pretty sure he had misheard her.

"She didn't tell you?" Valerie went on.

Melissa was gone. She'd left town. Without even a good-bye.

Aaron cleared his throat, trying to mask his shock. "I knew she'd be leaving at some point, but… I hoped I would catch her."

"You two looked like you were getting very cozy at the reception," Valerie said. "I can't imagine why she didn't tell you exactly when she was leaving."

"Me neither," Aaron muttered.

"Why don't you give her a call?"

Aaron nodded, and tried to keep his expression light. "Yeah. I'll do that." Then he extended the flowers. "Here. These are for you."

"Why, thank you, Aaron."

"You have a good day."

"Let me grab you a biscuit," Valerie offered. "You came all this way, and they're nice and fresh."

Aaron was about to protest, but smiled instead. "Sure. They smell delicious."

Valerie hurried off into the house and returned a short while later with a paper bag. As Aaron accepted it, he could tell that she'd put at least two biscuits inside. Maybe three. "Thank you so much, Mrs. Conwell."

Then he turned and started down the steps.

"Call Melissa, dear," Valerie said to him.

Aaron raised a hand as he headed down the walkway. "I will."

He got behind the wheel of his Mercedes, where he exhaled sharply. *Call Melissa...* The words were like a slap in the face.

Of course, Mrs. Conwell had no clue that he didn't have a way to reach her daughter. She'd given him that whole coy act about not giving him her number, making him believe that she wanted him to track her down the old-fashioned way.

Do a bit of chasing to prove to her that he was truly interested.

What a joke.

Was this her plan all along? To ditch him?

Aaron started his car.

Well, he wasn't about to be deterred so easily. Maybe this *was* a game. She expected him to pursue her, even if she wasn't making it easy.

All right. Game on.

Aaron eased his car into traffic. He was heading to Arlene's house.

Chapter 14

The thing with small towns was that pretty much everyone knew where everyone lived. And if you didn't know where a particular person resided, it wasn't hard to find out.

Aaron was well aware of Arlene's address. She lived right next to the town's original antique shop, where she happened to work. If he didn't find her at home, he would surely find her at the shop.

Ten minutes after leaving the Conwell residence, Aaron pulled up in front of the small turn-of-the century house that Arlene owned on the west side of Sheridan Falls. It was a two-story wood structure. An array of colorful flowers added to the curb appeal, and a fresh coat of white paint had the house looking new. As Aaron pulled his car to stop, he saw that Arlene was sitting on the porch, her young daughter blowing bubbles on the grass.

Aaron exited the car to find that Arlene had gotten to her feet. She was looking at him with curiosity. Her daughter, Raven, whom he'd met a handful of times in town with Arlene, ran over to him, clearly happy to have a visitor. "Do you want to try blowing some bubbles?"

Aaron humored her. "Sure." He took the little stick from her and the container, dipped it in, and blew out a stream of bubbles. Raven giggled happily as she chased and tried to catch them.

Arlene sauntered down the steps toward them. "Aaron," she said, looking at him oddly. "What brings you by?"

"You're not working today?" he asked.

"I needed a day off." Her lips curled in a faint smile, and Aaron sensed some weariness. "Is there something I can help you with?"

"I was hoping to find Melissa."

"Here? No, she's not here. In fact, I'm pretty sure she already left. But if not, you can find her at my parents' place."

"I've already been there."

Raven held up the stick for her mother. "Mommy, you try."

"You continue blowing bubbles, sweetie," Arlene said softly to her daughter. "Give me a moment to speak to Mr. Burke. I'll be over in a little while."

Raven blew some bubbles, then happily went off chasing them. Arlene faced Aaron again. "So she did leave."

"Apparently." The reality stung. Aaron hadn't thought she would leave town without seeing him again, or at least speaking to him. "I'm trying to track her down."

"Why don't you just call her?" Arlene asked.

The million-dollar question, which only drove home the point that he had been way off base with his thoughts about Melissa. He thought she'd *enjoyed* their time together. Hell, he knew she had. He'd assumed that enjoyment would lead her to want to see *more* of him. That wasn't an illogical thought, was it?

Never before had Aaron had such an incredible night with a woman, only for her to disappear from his life. Indeed, he had been the one to have to gently—and sometimes not so gently—push women away. He would start a relationship and quickly realize it wasn't what he wanted. The woman in question, while beautiful and seemingly sweet, would start dropping hints about some lavish item she wanted, or some would suggest they have sex without a condom. Aaron wasn't stupid. From personal experience, he knew that there were women who would try to ensnare a man with a pregnancy, whether he had a lot of money or not. He had been devastated by some of the truths he'd learned about Ella, and the lengths she'd gone to in order to manipulate him into getting what she wanted. It still hurt for him to think about what she'd done. Because of that painful experience, he knew that he had to be careful to pursue a woman interested in him, not in his wallet.

That hadn't been his concern with Melissa, given their history. But he had not for one moment entertained the thought that she would not only *not* chase him, but actually run from him.

They'd had an incredible night, and now she was gone? It didn't make sense.

"Well," Aaron began cautiously, "she forgot to give me her number."

"Really?" Was Aaron mistaken, or did Arlene look amused? "With all the time you spent together, you never exchanged the most basic information?"

"We were…busy. I thought she'd be around today."

"Well, it looks like you're out of luck, then."

Why did Arlene seem so happy about that fact? "I was hoping you could give me her number. I'd like to reach her."

"If my sister wanted you to be able to reach her, she would have given you her number."

Aaron looked at her askance. He offered her his most charming of smiles. "Come on. I only want a number. Not her address."

"If my sister didn't give you her number, there was a reason for that. Sorry. I have to respect her wishes."

To drive home the point that she wasn't kidding, Arlene turned and wandered over to her daughter. He heard her ask Raven about trying to blow some bubbles now.

"Arlene…"

She looked at him over her shoulder. "I guess a charming smile doesn't always get you what you want, does it? Even the Burke brothers have to deal with rejection."

"What's that supposed to mean?"

"Honestly, I was a bit surprised at how well you and Melissa connected at the reception," Arlene said. "I thought you burned the bridge on any sort of relationship with her years ago."

Aaron narrowed his eyes. "Is that what Melissa told you?"

"Okay, I'm going to try to blow the biggest bubble ever!" Arlene exclaimed, clearly ignoring him.

And with that, Aaron knew the conversation was over. He reached into his wallet and withdrew a business card. "Here, please give my number to Melissa. Tell her I'd like her to call me. Or email me. You give her my information, and she can make the choice to contact me or not."

Arlene took the card from him and gave it a brief glance. "Okay. But no promises she'll get in touch with you. Like I said, I think she would have left you her phone number if she wanted to stay in contact with you."

Aaron gave her a gracious smile, but he was irritated. First the comment about the Burke brothers. For some reason, people in this town thought he and his brothers believed they walked on water. It wasn't true. They'd earned that reputation when they were younger, and some of it was valid. But most of it was unfair judgment, simply because of who they were—Cyrus Burke's sons.

People in this town had put them on a pedestal, and Aaron hadn't asked to be there. Escaping to Europe to play professional soccer had been a relief. Living in a city where no one had known him as the son of a football superstar, he had been judged on his own merit. But ultimately, the pitfalls of fame had infected his life. A failed marriage, paparazzi lurking in the bushes when he was at restaurants, hoping to find something scandalous to write about him. Stories about him had filled the tabloids, whether or not there was a grain of truth to them.

Arlene's comment made him believe that she thought he loved the so-called perks of fame, but she had no clue. For every perk, there was a downside. Aaron truly enjoyed a quiet life and peace. When he'd retired from soccer last year and returned to Sheridan Falls, that had been his goal. He wanted to do something with meaning, which was why he'd started a charity to give back to children in need. He'd also hoped to have children of his own. But his marriage to Ella had quickly fallen apart once he was no longer whisking her on exotic vacations.

"Please, just give her my information," Aaron reiterated, hoping that Arlene would. "'Bye, Raven."

"'Bye!" She waved at him enthusiastically.

Aaron headed back to his vehicle. He wondered if some of Arlene's attitude was because she was bitter, having divorced Raven's father in what could only be described as a huge public scandal. In fact, it had been the biggest scandal in this town in a few years. Craig had not only cheated; he'd gotten another woman pregnant. The custody battle for Raven had only recently ended.

He hoped that Arlene wasn't so jaded that she would discourage her sister from pursuing a relationship with him.

A relationship? As Aaron started his car, he frowned at the direction of his thoughts. Was that what he wanted with Melissa?

He liked her. That's all he knew for sure. That spark he'd felt for her years ago was still there, and he wanted to get to know her all over again. See where things might lead. And if they led to more of what they'd enjoyed on Saturday night, then he was all for it.

Chapter 15

Three days later, Aaron was beyond frustrated. He hadn't heard from Melissa.

Now, sitting on his sofa with his laptop, he stared at the Twitter page for Turning Tides group home, where he'd learned that Melissa was the program director. That was one of the few things he'd been able to find out about her. When it came to social media, she was practically a ghost.

Aaron had found no Facebook profile, no personal Twitter. There was a LinkedIn profile, where he learned that she'd worked at Turning Tides for the past seven years. But any sort of personal information had been completely lacking.

She was leaving him no choice. He'd messaged her on LinkedIn days ago, and he'd gotten no response. He wouldn't be surprised to learn that she didn't check the app.

Now Aaron would have to contact the group home. Instead of calling—which was what he wanted to do—he would send a message through the website. A simple message asking that Melissa get back to him at her earliest convenience.

Hopefully this would finally get Melissa's attention.

"This looks amazing," Melissa said to Teresa, one of the counselors at the group home and her best friend. Her stomach grumbled as she eyed the macaroni topped with melted cheddar and bread crumbs, and the salad on the side. "The boys made this all on their own?"

"Well, I helped," Teresa said. "But this was entirely their idea, and they wanted to do a baked mac and cheese because you told them that's the only *real* mac and cheese."

Melissa smiled. "They remembered. Sometimes I wonder what gets through and what they instantly forget. Please tell them thank you. I don't have time right now to step away from my desk, not with my meeting in an hour."

"Will do," Teresa said. "Though I think you should take a break from your desk, even for fifteen minutes."

"I wish I could," Melissa said. "I've got too much work to do. I'm going over my notes for the plan of care meeting for Tyler. I'm still trying to reach his father, but he's out of town and hasn't gotten back to me." She sighed, then lifted the fork and spiked a cucumber in the salad. "No rest for the wicked."

And then she tried to suppress a smile as she thought about just how wicked she'd been—in Aaron's bed. The thought still made her smile almost a week later. So did the knowledge that Aaron had been trying to reach her. But Melissa held all the cards now. She hadn't gotten back to him.

Finally, he was getting a taste of his own medicine.

Melissa stuffed the cucumber into her mouth and turned her attention back to the computer when Teresa turned to leave the office.

"Oh, I almost forgot," Teresa said, and Melissa looked at her. "There's a message on the Twitter account for you. Did you see it?"

"What?"

"Someone named Aaron. Aaron Bradshaw. No, Aaron Burke. Said he's trying to reach you."

Though Melissa had just swallowed the cucumber, it felt as though it was suddenly lodged in her throat.

"I know you typically don't check the Twitter account, so I thought I'd ask. I'll screenshot the info and email it to you."

"Did he…say anything…specific?" Melissa asked, her heart thumping hard in her chest. She hoped Teresa couldn't sense her panic. But if Aaron had said anything that alluded to their night together…

Of course he hadn't, Melissa realized. If he had, Teresa would be grilling her for details.

"No," Teresa answered. "Do you know an Aaron? The message was so brief, I figured you must know him."

There was no point lying. "He's someone from Sheridan Falls. I saw him again at the wedding after several years. I guess he just wants to say hi."

Teresa nodded. "Oh, of course. I'll send you the information now."

Melissa forced a smile. "Great."

It didn't take more than a couple minutes for the email to come through. Melissa was barely breathing as she opened it.

Hello. This message is for Melissa Conwell. Please have her contact Aaron Burke at 716-555-8034. Or she can send an email to therealaaronburke@europeansportsonline.com.

Melissa blew out a slow breath. At least there'd been nothing suspicious in the message. Nothing for Teresa to give her the third degree about.

But still…

Melissa emitted a groan. She wanted to ignore the message. But given that he'd gone so far as to contact the group home looking for her, she was fairly certain that if she didn't respond to him, he would continue trying to reach her. Perhaps he'd even call the group home next.

She was glad that he'd provided his email address, because she didn't want to talk to him over the phone. Though she needed to continue getting ready for her upcoming meeting, Melissa quickly drafted an email to him.

Aaron, it's Melissa. Sorry I didn't get back to you sooner. I'm not really sure why you want to contact me. We had fun, and I appreciate that night more than you know. How-

ever, I'm not looking for anything to come from it. When
I'm back in Sheridan Falls, I'll be sure to say hello.

Melissa reread the email, wondering if she should change
it at all. It was direct and didn't sugarcoat anything. Perhaps
it was a little…tactless?

No, it was clear and to the point. She didn't want a relationship with him, so why give him the sweet version of
rejection that would have him still pursuing her? Better for
him to think she was a jerk and be done with her.

Besides, she had to get back to her preparation for the
plan of care meeting.

She quickly hit Send, then got back to work.

Aaron reread the email from Melissa, his stomach sink-
ing more with each passing second. He could hardly believe his eyes.

Had she really just given him a none-too-subtle brush-off?

Brush-off? Heck, she'd sent him a very clear "get lost"
message.

It didn't make sense.

Frowning, Aaron eased back on the sofa and ran a hand
over his head. He was baffled at the message. She'd spent
the night in his bed, begging for him to touch her here and
there, crying out his name, and *this* was what she sent him?

Aaron closed his laptop. He couldn't accept this message from her. *Wouldn't* accept it.

Had her sister gotten in her ear? Helped sour her opin-
ion of him? No, Aaron couldn't see that. Why would Ar-
lene do that? And Melissa was certainly her own person.
She wouldn't be swayed by someone else's biased opinion.
Because there wasn't anything negative Arlene could tell
Melissa about him that would be based in fact.

So something else was going on. But what?

Suddenly, a thought occurred to him. Something that

had his jaw tightening. It would definitely explain this bizarre reaction after they'd had such a great night together.

Had Melissa lied to him from the outset? The more
Aaron thought about it, the more he realized it was the
only thing that made sense.

Anger flared, hot and intense.

During his online search for anything about her, he'd
found a photo of her and some guy named Christopher
Fieldcote. They'd been out at some event in New York City,
and while the photo's caption didn't say they were a couple,
Melissa and this guy had looked pretty cozy.

Was he the reason for Melissa's email? Had she been
involved romantically with someone else and yet gone to
bed with him?

Aaron's pulse was pounding. He stood and walked to
the window in his living room. He looked out at the peace-
ful view of the trees in his front yard. But inside, he was
feeling the farthest thing from peace.

If Melissa had cheated on someone else with him, that
was unacceptable.

He needed to get to the bottom of this.

As soon as possible.

Dear Reader,

IT'S A FACT: if you answer 4 quick questions, we'll send you **4 FREE REWARDS!**

I'm not kidding you. As a leading publisher of women's fiction, we value your opinions... and your time. That's why we are prepared to **reward** you handsomely for completing our mini-survey. In fact, we have 4 Free Rewards for you, including 2 free books and 2 free gifts.

As you may have guessed, that's why our mini-survey is called **"4 for 4".** Answer 4 questions and get 4 Free Rewards. It's that simple!

Thank you for participating in our survey,

Pam Powers

To get your 4 FREE REWARDS:
Complete the survey below and return the insert today to receive 2 FREE BOOKS and 2 FREE GIFTS guaranteed!

"4 for 4" MINI-SURVEY

1 Is reading one of your favorite hobbies?
☐ YES ☐ NO

2 Do you prefer to read instead of watch TV?
☐ YES ☐ NO

3 Do you read newspapers and magazines?
☐ YES ☐ NO

4 Do you enjoy trying new book series with FREE BOOKS?
☐ YES ☐ NO

YES! I have completed the above Mini-Survey. Please send me my 4 FREE REWARDS (worth over $20 retail). I understand that I am under no obligation to buy anything, as explained on the back of this card.

168/368 XDL GMYK

FIRST NAME

LAST NAME

ADDRESS

APT.#

CITY

STATE/PROV.

ZIP/POSTAL CODE

Chapter 16

Melissa rubbed her pounding temple. "I don't think you're understanding me, Mr. Stone. Your son was not the victim in this situation. He was the instigator. He threw the first punch."

"He's there for you all to straighten him out. Why don't you do your job?"

Melissa inhaled a deep breath and counted to three. "I fully believe in your son, but he's acting out. I think if you were able to participate in the counseling sessions with him—"

"That's not possible," the man said curtly. "My business requires me to be in Europe for the next four weeks. Talk to his mother."

"I have spoken to his mother," Melissa said. "She's involved. But I think it would be especially meaningful if you could be here, too. Perhaps we can arrange to have you on Skype? I think it would mean a lot to—"

Melissa heard the man speaking, but his words were muffled. It took her a moment to realize that he wasn't speaking to her.

"I have a meeting I'm late for," Mr. Stone said. "We'll have to have this conversation another time."

"When would be a good time?" Melissa asked. But when she got no response, she realized that Mr. Stone had already hung up.

Melissa held the receiver in her hand and stared at it. She wanted to scream. How could Mr. Stone be so blind? Didn't he realize that his son needed him? Sure, Tyler had made some bad mistakes, but at his core he was a good kid. A kid who needed the presence of his dad in his life.

In Melissa's opinion, it was critical for Tyler's success that his father be involved in this process. In fact, she wouldn't be surprised to learn that Tyler's involvement with a gang and the robbery that got him arrested had been a cry for attention from a father who didn't make time for him.

Instead of being disappointed in his son for his mistakes, Mr. Stone needed to see his son's actions as a bid for attention and respond accordingly. Especially with his court case coming up in mere weeks. Tyler needed to be calm and not act out at the group home if he hoped to have a successful day in court.

She placed the receiver back on the cradle and rubbed her right temple. A migraine was starting. She opened her top desk drawer, withdrew the bottle of pain medication and took out two tablets. She washed them down with lukewarm coffee.

The knock on the door had her exhaling harshly. She just wanted a break. For a few glorious minutes, she wanted no distractions on this Friday afternoon.

But she sat up straight, tried to regain her composure, and said, "Come in."

The door opened, and Teresa peeked her head into the office. "I'm sorry," she began without preamble. "I know you said no unnecessary interruptions, but you have a visitor."

"The math tutor is here already?"

"No," Teresa responded simply, a look of intrigue in her eyes.

"Is it an emergency?"

"Sort of. He says he won't leave until you come out and speak to him."

"What's his name?"

"He refused to give me one. I tried to get him to make an appointment, but he wouldn't. Honestly, I'd be more alarmed if he weren't so darned attractive."

Melissa frowned. "He's cute?"

"Very."

Melissa's pulse quickened. It couldn't be…no, the thought was crazy. It wouldn't be Aaron.

"But he does seem a little upset," Teresa said. "Well, maybe upset is the wrong word. He seems…focused. I think you need to come out and talk to him. I'll keep my phone on hand in case I need to call the police."

Unsure what to make of Teresa's announcement, Melissa pushed her chair back and stood. Could it be Christopher? He'd called her a few times recently, asking if they could talk. No, Teresa should know what Christopher looked like. Even though she'd never met him in person, she'd seen a couple of photos of him.

Following Teresa out of the office, Melissa made her way down the hall that led to the front of the house. She heard the frantic pounding of footsteps racing up the staircase, then Omar yelled, "Hey, everyone—come downstairs!"

What was going on?

A couple seconds later, when she stepped out from behind the staircase and saw who was standing in the foyer, her heart leaped into her throat. Her eyes bulged, and she stopped midstep.

No…it couldn't be…

Her eyes flitted from Aaron, who somehow was here in her place of work, to Omar, who had just bounded down the stairs. Her stunned gaze went to Aaron again. His taut shoulders relaxed, and he smiled at her.

"What haven't you told me?" Teresa whispered. "Because you know him, don't you? Are you seeing this guy?"

"Aaron," Melissa said, her voice barely more than a whisper. Tyler, Mohammad and Ben raced down the stairs, huge smiles on their faces. "What are you doing here?"

"I knew it!" Omar exclaimed. "You're Aaron Burke!"

Aaron grinned at the boys. "Yes. Yes, I am."

There was a chorus of excitement, with exclamations

like "Whoa!" and "For real!" and "Oh my God!" The boys immediately began to high-five and hug him.

"You're seeing him, aren't you?" Teresa demanded in a hushed voice as the boys swarmed Aaron.

"No, I'm not," Melissa responded, giving Teresa a pointed look. This was *not* something she wanted to discuss right now.

Aaron held up a hand, saying, "I take it you guys like soccer?"

"I'm a huge fan," Omar exclaimed. He was grinning from ear to ear.

Melissa stepped closer to Aaron and his throng of admirers, anger making her face flush. This was not appropriate. Aaron should not have shown up here like this and caused a disruption to the day. There were routines here, work that needed to be done. Sure, it was a lunch break now, but the boys were supposed to be in the backyard getting exercise, not crowding the lobby.

What had Aaron been thinking?

"Boys, you know this is time for physical activity," Melissa pointed out.

"But this is Aaron Burke!"

"I know exactly who he is," Melissa said.

She faced Aaron now, her eyes letting him know that she wasn't pleased with this intrusion.

"Wait—you know him?" Tyler asked.

"Duh, obviously she knows him. That's why he's here," Ben said.

Before Melissa could speak, Aaron did. "Ms. Conwell and I go way back."

"Cool!"

"Awesome!"

"Are you her boyfriend?"

Melissa's heart began to race. How would Aaron answer that last question?

She couldn't let him, so she spoke quickly. "Mr. Burke and I knew each other when we were kids," she said. "He's...he's in town and decided to visit me," she added by way of explanation. "But no, he's not my boyfriend."

"Aw."

The chorus of disappointment surprised her. As did the look of discontent on Teresa's face.

Melissa glanced at Aaron, saw him give her a questioning look. Was he actually disputing the fact that they weren't an item?

Melissa hoped that neither the boys nor Teresa had picked up on that subtle look. Yes, she'd slept with him. But just because she had didn't mean they were an item. After all, they'd slept together twelve years ago, and that had meant nothing to Aaron.

Their wedding fling was just that—a fling, the kind of thing Melissa was certain happened all the time. She had scratched an itch. Satisfied her curiosity. She'd had a great night, but that's all it was. One night.

"Chase is gonna be *so* upset when he learns you were here," Omar said. "He's out with Counselor Mike right now. How long are you staying?"

"Not long," Melissa quickly interjected. "Mr. Burke, will you follow me?" She was trying her best to maintain a professional tone with him. Desperate to not have anyone think there might be anything suspicious going on between them.

"I'd love to," Aaron said.

Melissa led the way down the hallway and around the corner to her office at the back of the house. She opened the door and headed inside, and Aaron followed her. She closed the door behind him and faced him.

"What are you doing here?" she asked. Gone was the professional and dispassionate tone. Her heart was beating fast. She didn't understand what Aaron was doing here, especially after the message she'd sent him yesterday.

"You're a hard woman to reach," he said.

"Why did you come all the way to New Jersey?"

"After the email you sent me, I figured you owe me an explanation."

Melissa raised an eyebrow. "You couldn't ask it via email? Or call me?"

"You have a way of not responding that makes it challenging for guy to get in touch with you," he said, giving her a pointed look.

Melissa couldn't say anything to that, because it was true. She'd been avoiding him. If only she'd known that he would show up here, she would have answered his calls. And she definitely wouldn't have sent that email.

And now that he'd shown up here, she knew she wouldn't live this one down. Teresa would have questions, and of course the boys would be speculating as well.

"Besides," Aaron went on, "this is something I wanted to ask you in person."

"What could you possibly want to ask me that would have you coming here? To my place of work?"

"Why did you send me that email?"

Melissa crossed her arms over her chest. "Are you so unaccustomed to rejection that you flew out here to demand an explanation?"

"Rejection doesn't typically start with a woman clinging to me so tightly in my bed that she practically leaves scars on my back."

Melissa's face flamed. She quickly turned, unable to face him.

"Oh, no, no, no. You're not going to avoid this one." Aaron scooted in front of her. "I need to see your eyes when you answer me."

"We had a great night," Melissa said in a lowered voice,

hoping to God that no one was lurking outside her door in the hallway. "But it was one night. Surely you've had a one-night stand before."

"You don't strike me as the type to engage in a one-night stand."

"As if you know anything about me," Melissa quipped.

Aaron blew out a frazzled breath. "What are you doing tonight?"

Melissa narrowed her eyes as she looked at him. *That* was his follow-up question? "What?"

"Tell me," he said.

"I am so confused right now."

"So am I," Aaron said. "Now answer my question."

She could tell by the sternness in his voice that he wasn't going to drop the issue. But if he had some bizarre notion that she was going to spend the night with him, he had another think coming.

"I have plans," Melissa said. Though the only plan she actually had was to head home and take a hot bath, drink a glass of wine and perhaps watch a movie before going to bed.

"With Christopher?" Aaron took a step toward her, his eyes boring into hers. "Is he the reason why you've given me the brush-off?"

Chapter 17

Melissa stared into Aaron's hard gaze, momentarily caught off guard. Christopher...?

And then it hit her, and her eyes bulged. Somehow, Aaron knew that she had been dating a man named Christopher. But how?

"I need to know," Aaron said. "Is Christopher the reason you've been avoiding me? Is he your boyfriend?"

"How do you even know about Christopher?" Had he hired someone to look into her life?

"So you *are* seeing him," Aaron surmised. Then he swore under his breath.

He looked upset, something Melissa didn't expect. Did he actually care, or was this about his ego being hurt?

She could let him believe that she was involved with Christopher, though their brief relationship had ended eight months earlier. Maybe it would be easier this way. If Aaron thought she was involved with another man, he would leave her alone once and for all...

And yet she found herself saying, "No. Christopher and I are no longer involved."

Aaron stared at her long and hard, as if trying to decide whether or not he believed her. After several moments, his features relaxed.

This *had* been bothering him. Melissa was confused.

"So he's not the reason you sent me that email?" Aaron asked.

"No."

"And what about another guy? Are you dating someone?"

"You said you didn't think I was the type to engage in a one-night stand. Now you think I'm the type to sleep with you while I have a boyfriend?"

"Wine, music, a lapse in judgment. People do it all the time."

"I don't," Melissa said, unable to hide her irritation.

"Good." Aaron paused. "Because I need you to be my date tonight."

Melissa's eyes widened, even as her heart skipped a beat. "That's quite presumptuous of you."

"It's an event I hope you'll be willing to attend with me. It's for a good cause."

More like an excuse to get me naked again, she thought. Though she had herself to blame for Aaron believing that he could wiggle a finger and seduce her again. She'd been a far too eager participant last Saturday night.

"What is this good cause?" she asked, trying her best to keep her doubt from creeping into her voice.

"I'm in town for a charity fund-raiser tonight," Aaron explained. "Have you heard about a little girl named Rosella Nunez?"

The name sounded familiar. And in an instant it came to her. "Yes, that little girl who needs a liver. She's only two years old, and she's going to die if she doesn't have a transplant soon."

"Yes, that's her. Well, her father is a huge soccer fan. I know some of the guys who play for the New York Red Bulls. The team's actually based out of Jersey, right nearby in Harrison."

"Yes, that's a suburb of Newark," Melissa said.

"Anyway, some of the players heard about Rosella's plight and suggested holding a fund-raiser for the family. It's a tough situation. The parents have had to quit their jobs in order to provide round-the-clock care for Rosella, and they've exhausted almost every penny they have for medical care. Obviously this is a trying time for the family, and the fund-raiser tonight is to help lessen their financial burden. I was hoping you would accompany me as my date."

Darn it. Melissa had been prepared to shut down whatever Aaron might have asked her. But now, how could she?

She'd heard about this young girl. It was a heartbreaking story, and certainly the most worthy of causes. As much as Melissa wanted to refuse to be Aaron's date, his story about the fund-raiser changed everything.

"And this is actually tonight?" she asked.

"Yes."

"Jeez, you don't give a girl much notice."

Aaron raised an eyebrow. "I would have—if you'd responded to me."

Melissa said nothing. What could she say?

Aaron wandered toward the window and looked out at the backyard. His face lit up in a smile, and he waved.

The kids must have been looking up at the window, fascinated that Aaron Burke, real-life soccer star, was here.

"You really are a big star," Melissa commented.

"Did you follow my career?" Aaron asked, facing her. "Or did you forget about me?"

"I…" She swallowed. "It was all but impossible to hear nothing of your success," Melissa said. "Everything you do is big news in Sheridan Falls."

"I see."

What did he see? Was he offended that she hadn't become his biggest fan?

"I love that you ended up working with kids," Aaron said, once again glancing outside. "Just like we used to back in the day."

Melissa's jaw stiffened. She didn't want to hear him talk about that—the very thing that had helped them forge a bond twelve years ago.

"Why would you *love* that I ended up working with kids? Why does anything we used to do *back in the day* matter to you?"

"Okay, so there it is," Aaron said. "You're upset with me because of how things ended."

"One day everything was great, the next thing you were pushing me away."

"I was young. I didn't want to hold you back."

"How would you hold me back?" Melissa asked. She hadn't planned on having this conversation with Aaron, but the breakup had weighed heavily on her heart. She wanted answers. "I wanted to be with you. Why wasn't I good enough?"

"Is that what you think?"

"What am I supposed to think? And then you married *Ella*. Of all people."

"It's not you who wasn't good enough," Aaron said, and pain flashed in his eyes.

Melissa waited for him to go on, but he didn't. Instead, he turned away from her.

Something hit her then as she heard his heavy breath. Was he still carrying guilt over his young sister's death? The night they'd made love, Aaron had confided in her that he'd been torn up with guilt for years because Chantelle had drowned when he had been watching her.

"Chantelle," Melissa said softly. "You still feel guilt over her death."

"It was my fault."

Was this why he'd broken up with her? Melissa knew from working with troubled youth that sometimes when people experienced a tragedy, they were emotionally stuck—unable to move forward and be happy because guilt held them back.

Melissa was gentle when she asked, "Did you push me away because of Chantelle?"

Aaron turned to face her. "I don't want to talk about Chantelle."

"But if you're still holding yourself responsible—"

"What I said twelve years ago doesn't matter," Aaron said, and the firm tone of his voice made it clear he didn't want to discuss the issue further. "Will you go out with me tonight?"

So he was going to avoid the subject. He was sounding like the Aaron he'd been just before they'd broken up, when she sensed something was wrong and he'd refused to talk to her about what was bothering him.

That was the man who'd hurt her. If he still wasn't willing to open up to her, clearly he would hurt her again.

If she let him. The more time she spent with him, the worse it was going to be for her. She needed to end this, whatever it was, before it went any further.

"You know what?" she began. "I'm not sure I can make it tonight. I do appreciate that it's a great cause and that you came here to invite me. But it's such last-minute notice. I'll happily give a donation, however."

"I want you there with me."

The commanding tone to Aaron's voice caused Melissa's heart to flutter. Gone was the vulnerable man from just a few minutes earlier. Despite herself, she liked his determination. It had always been one of his most attractive qualities. Still, she didn't want to spend any more time with him. She drew in a breath, then said, "I don't have a single decent thing to wear."

"You don't need to worry about that," Aaron told her.

"Look at me." She spread her arms wide so that he could get a good look at her simple blouse, jeans and flats. "This is my typical wardrobe. Not nearly appropriate for a fancy shindig with lots of well-to-do high-society people. Maybe you can ask someone else."

"You're the only one I want to ask."

Melissa bit her bottom lip as he held her gaze. God, that look. It would be her undoing. She could see the heat in his eyes, as well as his determination. He wanted her in his bed again.

She'd already allowed herself one night with Aaron, one night that was to be her last. So going out with him tonight was a very bad idea.

"It's practically in your backyard," Aaron said. "And you don't have a boyfriend. Nothing to stop you from going with me."

"What if I just don't want to spend more time with you?" she found herself saying.

Aaron closed the distance between them in a flash. "You don't?" The question was a challenge. "Is that what you're telling me?"

Melissa gulped.

"Because I find it hard to believe you faked your attraction for me last weekend. And suddenly you're done with me?"

Heat zapped Melissa's body. She hadn't faked her attraction. Not at all. But she needed to protect her sanity. Spending more time with Aaron was a bad idea.

So she said, "Aaron, I would go, but honestly I don't want to go in any old thing. You have to trust me when I say I don't have the right kind of dress."

"I already told you, you don't have to worry about that."

"I don't understand how you can say that."

"Before I came here, I made a stop. The wife of one of the guys who plays for the Red Bulls owns a boutique. I stopped by and took a look at what she had. There's an outfit that I think would look incredible on you."

Melissa shot him a skeptical look. "Why would you go to a store to look for an outfit for me if you thought I had a boyfriend?"

"Because my gut told me you didn't." He held her gaze. "Not after the night we shared."

Melissa's face flamed.

"It's red," Aaron said, his voice husky.

Red…like the outfit she'd worn the night of the welcome dinner.

"Red looks incredible on you," he told her, stroking her face.

"Aaron, you can't—" Melissa took a step backward. "Someone could come in here right now."

"I need you with me tonight," he said, and Melissa could hear the yearning in his voice.

Her womb tightened. God help her, she was all but putty in Aaron's hands when she was around him. Why couldn't her brain take over and prevent her body from betraying her?

"You seriously picked out a dress for me?" she asked.

"I seriously did. And accessories. Everything you need to go along with the dress will be available for you at the shop. Though I'd really love for you to wear those shoes you wore with your red dress last week," he added in a low voice.

A shiver of delight danced down Melissa's spine.

"You're going to be the most beautiful woman in the room. Even if you go just as you are right now."

Melissa's resolve softened. "Aaron…"

"I took the liberty of making an appointment for you," he said. "Five o'clock. You'll get dressed at the store, and I can meet you there to pick you up. Then we can make it into New York for the event, which starts at seven-thirty. I'm looking forward to this night being one that the Nunez family will never forget."

Despite herself, a wave of excitement shot through Melissa. Aaron had actually gone to a boutique to pick out a dress for her? It was the kind of thing that she would never expect a man to do. Aaron was exhibiting a take-charge attitude, the kind that Melissa always thought she wouldn't like. But the truth was, it was kind of thrilling…

Aaron had come here with a plan. A plan to take her out and not take no for an answer. She felt a stirring of desire. What would it hurt to spend another night with him?

"All right," she said.

"I can pick you up and take you to the boutique, if you like."

"There's no need. I can get there on my own, and you can meet me there once I'm dressed. Let's say five thirtyish?"

Aaron's face lit up with a smile. "That'll work."

For a nanosecond, Melissa couldn't help thinking that she was giving Aaron exactly what he wanted. He'd come here with one goal in mind: to take her out, and she was certain that he didn't expect to take no for an answer. He'd succeeded in his goal with barely any resistance from her.

Because she wanted the same thing. Just seeing Aaron again had her body remembering their chemistry. The hot sex.

And now he was offering her another night out together, another evening where they would get dressed up to the nines, have a glass of wine. Maybe two.

Would they end the night making love again?

Did a zebra have stripes?

Melissa glanced at the clock. "It's one o'clock. I can probably get out of here around three thirty, head home and shower, get ready. Then I can head to the boutique."

"But you'll have to leave your car there." Aaron pursed his lips. "Why don't I have a car pick you up at your place and drop you off at the store? The driver can then get me, then swing back to the store for you."

Melissa nodded. "I guess that makes the most sense."

"All right," Aaron said. "I'll need your contact information, then."

"Okay."

"Start with your phone number," he told her, giving her a knowing smile.

Chapter 18

Melissa was hoping that Aaron could escape the group home unnoticed, but he'd barely made it out of her office before the boys were there, swarming him. Soon, someone was suggesting that he play a game of soccer with them in the backyard.

"I think Aaron has to go," Melissa said.

"Aw," Omar, the oldest of the boys, protested. Then he looked at Aaron and said, "Please, can't you stay a little while longer?"

"I've got a bit of time," Aaron said. There were cheers of excitement, and two of the boys took Aaron by the arm and led him toward the back patio door. He wore dress pants and shoes, not the proper attire to kick a ball around, but he followed the boys outside nonetheless.

Melissa watched them go, then headed to the back door and looked outside. The excited expressions on the boys' faces made her smile. It was nice to see them so happy.

Someone tossed Aaron the soccer ball, and he immediately started to do some fancy footwork with it, bouncing the ball first off his foot, then his knee. The ball went high, and he dipped his head to hit it, knocking it forward.

He made what he'd just done look easy, but Melissa knew it took skill. Omar tried to follow Aaron's example and failed. But Aaron passed the ball back, and with a huge smile, Omar tried again.

"So," Teresa said, and Melissa realized that her friend was directly beside her. Melissa glanced at her, saw that Teresa was looking out the window at the star of the hour. "Who is he and why have I not heard about him before?"

Melissa released a shuddery breath. "That's Aaron Burke."

"The guy who emailed you yesterday. Why is he here? Why did he come to see you?"

Melissa gazed out the window in time to see Aaron kicking the ball to Tyler and the boys racing through the backyard. He was making some sort of hand gestures, and the boys seemed to separate into two makeshift teams.

Even just observing him for these few minutes, it was easy to tell that Aaron was really good with kids. She wondered why he and Ella had never had any.

Just the thought of Ella caused a bitter taste to fill her mouth. She met Teresa's curious gaze and tried her best to manage a neutral expression. "I grew up with Aaron Burke. And…years ago we used to date."

"What!" Teresa's eyes grew wide. "You used to date that *fine* brother?"

"It was a summer fling," Melissa said, trying to minimize their affair. But the truth was, she had never felt as though it was simply a summer affair. It had meant a whole lot more to her.

"Wait," Teresa said, and her eyes lit up, as though something had just occurred to her. "He was at the wedding last weekend. And you two hooked up, didn't you?"

Melissa said nothing.

"Don't bother denying it," Teresa said. "I told you you looked different when you got back from Sheridan Falls. Didn't I say that? I told you that you looked…*relaxed*." Teresa chuckled. "Now I get it."

"It's not a big deal," Melissa said. She knew there was no point in lying. Teresa wouldn't believe her. "I hooked up with an old flame." She shrugged. "It happens all the time at weddings."

Teresa's eyes grew as wide as saucers. "No big deal? When was the last time you had sex?"

Melissa crossed her arms over her chest. "It's not like I'm in the running for woman who's gone the longest without sex. And can you keep your voice down? I don't want anyone hearing this."

"All the boys are outside with Aaron, and Dana and Courtney are meeting with that probation officer. No one's going to hear."

Teresa was right. Melissa was being paranoid, but she didn't want to talk about last weekend.

"So why did he come here? Obviously the sex last weekend had to be amazing!"

"He's in town for a charity event," Melissa said. Then she explained the details. "He wants me to be his date."

Teresa's eyes were practically dancing with glee. "So this is already getting serious!"

"The event happens to be in New York, and I happen to be right here in Newark. It's convenient."

"I'm sure he could have asked anyone else to go with him. And he could certainly have flown the date of his choice here if he wanted to."

You're the only one I want to ask...

"It's a charity event. Not a romantic date."

Teresa smirked. "Whatever. Talk to me tomorrow. Just don't leave out any of the juicy details."

Melissa's first wow moment of the evening came when the Maybach arrived to pick her up. She'd thought Aaron would send a regular limo, or perhaps a regular sedan. But a Maybach? The most expensive of the Mercedes line?

He wasn't in the car, and she wondered where he was getting ready.

It really hit her that she was about to have her own *Pretty Woman* type of moment in a boutique when the driver stopped in front of *Dazzle*. Just looking at the storefront, she could tell it was very high-end. The kind of store Melissa wouldn't normally step in, because a dress could easily cost her a year's salary.

But here she was. This was really happening.

The driver exited the vehicle, made his way to the back

door and opened it for her. There was a smiling woman standing just inside the boutique, behind a Closed sign, and as Melissa approached, she opened the door for her.

"You must be Melissa," she said, extending a hand.

Melissa shook it. "Yes."

"I'm Crystal."

"Very nice to meet you," Melissa said. "Thanks so much for having me. I didn't realize I'm coming after hours."

"Actually, I closed the shop for you. Aaron insisted. He wanted you to have my undivided attention as you got ready. And he's made it worth my while, trust me."

Given the smile on Crystal's face, Melissa could only imagine. And it made her feel warm and fuzzy inside. Aaron was certainly pulling out all the stops for her.

Crystal began to walk, and Melissa fell into step beside her. "I think you're going to love the dress Aaron picked for you. It's right there."

They rounded the corner into the dressing room area, and when Melissa saw the dress hanging on the dressing room door, she stopped dead in her tracks.

"Oh my God," she uttered. "That's the dress?"

Crystal grinned from ear to ear. "Yep."

It was an off-the-shoulder trumpet gown made of red satin. The neckline was adorned with black lace and black jewels. The same lace and jewels were also embedded around the dress's waist. It looked formfitting and flared outward at the knee.

It was gorgeous.

Melissa had wondered if her pumps would work with this dress, but the combination of black and red on the dress would match her shoes perfectly.

"Try it on," Crystal urged.

With an excited giggle, Melissa headed into the changing room. The look on Crystal's face said it all once Melissa had the dress on. Her mouth formed a perfect O and her eyes lit up.

"You look stunning."

Melissa made her way to the large wall of floor-to-ceiling mirrors, and when she saw her reflection, her heart fluttered. She *did* look stunning. How had Aaron picked out the perfect dress for her?

Red looks incredible on you...

"I already picked out some accessories that I think would look fabulous with this gown," Crystal said. "A necklace made with onyx jewels, and a matching bracelet. Would you like to try them on?"

"Yes, please."

Once Melissa had the entire outfit on, including her shoes, she was mesmerized by how incredible she looked. She'd curled her hair and pinned it up, and Crystal helped her finesse the look.

Melissa noted that neither of the items she'd tried on had a price tag, but she knew this must cost a small fortune.

"Am I supposed to keep all of this?" Melissa asked, gently stroking the teardrop onyx stone.

"It's all for you," Crystal said. "A gift from Aaron." Pausing for a moment, Crystal smiled. "He's a great guy. My husband has known him since college, and he has nothing but high praise for him. And from what I can see, he likes you. A lot."

Melissa expelled a shuddery breath. She couldn't wait to see the look on Aaron's face when he saw her in this dress.

Aaron arrived at the shop and exited the limo, anxious to see Melissa. He already knew she would look amazing, but the text from Crystal had him extra excited.

Wait until you see her!

Aaron didn't have to wait long. Within a few seconds, he saw Crystal heading toward the door. She opened it wide, and then Melissa came into view.

A slow breath oozed out of Aaron. "Wow."

Melissa's face lit up in a smile. God, she was a vision of loveliness. The red dress hugged her curvaceous hips and her bountiful bosom. She was gorgeous, classy and sexy all at the same time.

Aaron wanted more than anything to take her in his arms and kiss her until she begged him to skip the event. He wanted to smooth his hands over those curvy hips.

He wanted her.

"Hi," she said, her voice wavering.

Aaron finally stepped toward her. "You look incredible."

"Thank you," she said, and twirled so that he could see the entire dress.

"And you're wearing the shoes?" he asked softly.

She lifted the hem of the dress so that he could see. "Yes."

"Oh, your bag," Crystal said, then disappeared into the store.

"Honestly, you're the most beautiful woman in the world," Aaron said. He leaned down and gave Melissa a soft kiss on the lips.

He saw the way her chest rose with the deep inhalation of breath. Was she as happy to see him as he was to see her?

"You don't have to say that," Melissa whispered.

"Did you look in a mirror?" Aaron countered. "I'm going to be the envy of the ball," he added with a playful smile.

Crystal returned with a tote bag. She passed it to Melissa. "Your belongings."

"Thanks," Melissa said.

Aaron took the bag from Melissa. "Crystal, thanks so much for everything," he said.

"Any time. You two have fun."

Then he offered Melissa his elbow, and she took it. He walked with her the short distance to the Maybach and opened the door, and she got in. He put her bag in the trunk, then got into the back seat beside her and took her hand.

She glanced at him and gave him a little smile.

Damn, she looked incredible. Aaron was seriously tempted to tell the driver to head straight back to his hotel.

But he would wait. And the waiting would make it all the more exciting.

Chapter 19

The ballroom at the Waldorf Astoria was the most spectacular room Melissa had ever seen. The walls were illuminated in pale pink, and trees with tiny crystal lights were strategically placed around the room. The tablecloths were accented in gold, and gold candles sat in glass containers. Melissa felt as though she had walked onto the set of a fairy tale.

The various items listed for the silent auction were placed on tables around the perimeter of the room. Jewelry sets. Paintings. Sports paraphernalia. Unique art sculptures. Weekend getaways. There was an amazing lineup of items to bid on.

And the people she'd met so far were absolutely lovely. Melissa had assumed that the crowd of high-profile citizens would be stuffy and conceited, but to her surprise, they were kind and friendly.

"Hey, gorgeous," Aaron said, slipping a hand around her waist. "See anything you like?"

"So much of it is amazing," Melissa said. "And I saw that you donated your original soccer jersey."

"It was the least I could do. I hope it fetches a pretty penny."

"Let's hope." Melissa turned toward the item she was standing in front of. "I'm really drawn to this painting by Felix Virgo." She angled her head as she looked at the painting of a swan peacefully swimming on a lake among lily pads. "It's so serene. I'd love to have this hanging on my office wall. Just looking at it would give me a sense of calm."

"It's beautiful," Aaron agreed. He looked into Melissa's eyes. "And so are you."

His unexpected compliment caused her stomach to flutter. "Thank you."

"Seriously, you're the most beautiful woman here." He slipped his arm around her waist.

Melissa cleared her throat. "Um…should we be doing this here?"

"I don't see why not," Aaron told her.

Heat coursed through Melissa's veins. Being this close to Aaron, she thought she might lose her mind. "I can hardly concentrate on the auction items with you near me," she whispered.

Aaron beamed, seemingly amused by her answer. "I'll leave you to mingle in peace."

With that, Aaron turned and made his way into the crowd, and Melissa saw him almost immediately hug another athlete—no doubt another soccer player.

"Hello."

Melissa turned to look at the woman who'd sidled up beside her. She was beautiful, with an olive complexion, her dark hair styled in an elegant chignon. She had bright eyes and a big smile.

"Hello," Melissa returned.

"I'm Olivia Rivera," she said, and extended a hand.

"Melissa Conwell." She shook the woman's hand.

"You're here with Aaron Burke."

Obviously, the woman was stating a fact, not asking a question. But Melissa responded anyway. "Yes."

"It's nice to see Aaron dating again."

"Oh, we're not dating. We're friends. We go way back."

"Hmm." Olivia's eyes narrowed slightly, as though she was confused by Melissa's answer. "Well, it's nice to see Aaron out regardless. After things fell apart with Ella, we didn't see him for a while."

"I guess you're one of the soccer wives," Melissa surmised.

"Yes. I'm married to Antonio Rivera. He and Aaron

played for the LA Galaxy for a couple of years before Aaron went off to Europe. We were all very happy for Aaron's success."

Melissa nodded. "This is a great event."

"Yes. Lovely venue, and I'm sure a lot of money will be raised for the Nunez family."

Once again, Melissa couldn't help thinking that her judgment had been way off regarding the people who would be here tonight. When she'd first walked into this ballroom on Aaron's arm, she'd assumed that everyone would be stuck-up and accustomed to adoration. Instead, Melissa had found down-to-earth people who cared about the cause.

Seeing the slideshow of the young girl at the start of the night and hearing about the family's terrible struggles had really touched Melissa. She checked out many of the other items up for bids but found herself wandering back to the painting by Felix Virgo. She didn't know why, but looking at this picture made her feel good.

She lifted the pen and scrawled her bid onto the paper. It was a hefty amount, but it was for a good cause.

She hoped her bid would be enough to secure the painting.

Aaron watched Melissa from across the room. Two men were talking to her, and they looked enthralled.

Aaron couldn't blame them. Melissa was utterly ravishing.

And he couldn't wait a minute longer. He needed to get her out of this room. Now.

Aaron had a suite booked upstairs. And that's where he wanted to be with Melissa. Holding her, kissing her, making sweet love to her.

He crossed the room toward her. As if sensing him, she turned, and a smile lit up her face.

God, she was radiant. And in the outfit she was wearing, she was easily the most beautiful woman in the room.

"Aaron," she said. The two men standing with her parted, allowing Aaron to close the distance between him and Melissa. He bit down on his bottom lip as he looked at her. What he really wanted to be doing was biting down on her lips. He wanted to take her in his arms in front of this crowd and kiss her senseless. Kiss her until she begged him to make love to her.

He slipped an arm around her waist, pulled her close and whispered in her ear, "Let's get out of here."

"We're not going to wait until they announce the winners of the auction?"

"They'll let us know if we won anything." He tightened his grip on her. "I need to take you upstairs. Now."

Melissa's eyelids fluttered. She looked up at him with those beautiful doe eyes. Beneath that wide-eyed gaze, he could see her passion. And he could also sense her hesitation. The same hesitation that he'd gotten from her when he'd shown up at her place of work.

Their connection was fiery, and Aaron wasn't afraid of it. He didn't want Melissa to be afraid of it, either.

He wanted to brand her, make her his. He wanted to give her all of him.

"You're sure?" Melissa asked.

"Do you know how absolutely irresistible you are?" he asked.

"People are probably staring," Melissa whispered.

"All the more reason to get out of here now."

He took her by the hand and looked into her eyes, where he saw no more hesitation.

"Okay," she said softly.

Aaron whisked her out of the ballroom.

Melissa felt a rush of excitement as Aaron led her to the elevator. They were a respectable couple as they waited for the elevator to arrive, but once they were inside, and alone, Aaron swept her into his arms and planted his lips on hers.

His lips moved over hers hungrily, and his hands roamed over her back. His tongue tangling with hers, their heavy breaths filled the enclosed space until the ping of the elevator sounded. They came apart quickly, and Melissa was relieved to see that they were on Aaron's floor.

Still, that didn't mean that no one was about to enter the elevator.

But when the doors opened, no one was there. Aaron quickly took Melissa's hand and led her down the hallway. She giggled as she had to jog to keep up with Aaron's fast pace.

The electricity between them sizzled. She loved the way she felt when he looked into her eyes—the thrill of excitement that came from knowing just how much he wanted her.

Aaron opened the door, and Melissa entered the suite first. He quickly followed her inside, flicking the light switch on.

He pulled her into his arms, his lips coming down on hers before he'd even closed the door. Melissa sighed as his tongue delved into her mouth.

A lingering groan rumbled in Aaron's chest, and a sexual charge shot through Melissa. Knowing that he was turned on so much that he couldn't even wait until the end of the event to get her upstairs excited her even more. She looped her arms around his neck and held on, her legs growing weak as she succumbed to his sensual assault on her lips.

"Baby," Aaron whispered, and he brought a hand to her face. Softly, he stroked her skin, then cupped her cheek. All the while he was moving with her, walking her backward into the living room of the suite. Several seconds later, her legs ran into the sofa, and she stumbled. Aaron held her and gently guided her down onto the chaise lounge, then went down on top of her, holding his strong frame above her so that he didn't hurt her. Melissa straightened her body out on the sofa, and Aaron stretched his strong, masculine body over hers.

He kissed her jawline, then dipped his mouth beneath her jaw, to her neck. He skimmed her flesh with those beautiful, full lips of his, causing a ripple of delicious sensations to swirl through her.

Then his head went lower, and he planted soft kisses on her collarbone before trailing his lips to the area above her breasts. Melissa caressed his head as he softly suckled the flesh of her cleavage. Her internal body temperature was rising rapidly.

Aaron lifted his head and looked into her eyes. "Every time I touch you, I go crazy."

His words made her shudder. The way he was stroking her skin, the way he was gazing at her... Melissa felt like the only woman in the world. "Every time you touch me, you make me crazy," she told him, her voice but a whisper.

"Tell me you were thinking about this the moment you saw me today. Tell me you wanted to make love to me as badly as I wanted to make love to you..."

His voice held a pleading tone, as if it would crush him to hear anything other than that Melissa desired and wanted him as much as he did her.

"Yes," she rasped, meaning it. "I couldn't help thinking about you kissing me again. Making love to me again..."

"Oh, baby..." Aaron moaned. He kissed her deeply, his tongue tangling with hers. Melissa snaked her foot around the back of Aaron's thigh as much as her skirt would allow.

"As beautiful as this dress is, I need to get you out of it."

He got to his feet and pulled her to a standing position. Melissa immediately reached for the zipper beneath her right arm and pulled it down. She shimmied out of the dress and stood before Aaron in only her strapless bra and lacy underwear.

"Take it all off for me, baby," he rasped. "Except for the shoes. I love those shoes."

Turned on by his words, Melissa quickly undid her bra and tossed it onto the floor. Then she pushed her underwear over her hips and down her thighs and kicked them aside.

Fully undressed, she met Aaron's gaze. His eyes were darkened with lust.

His gaze was like a caress, sweeping over her from head to toe. He expelled an audible breath. "Oh, baby."

Melissa swallowed. She was a little self-conscious standing in front of Aaron like this, fully exposed, totally vulnerable. But as he stepped toward her, the obvious desire in his eyes melted away her insecurity. She was no longer thinking about her body's flaws.

"You're perfect," Aaron told her.

He spoke as though he was seeing her naked for the first time. As though they hadn't been naked and getting it on just last week. Those lips had already explored every inch of her body.

He pulled her into his arms and brought his lips down on hers. This time, the kiss was slow and hot, causing every inch of her body to tingle. Her hands encircling his neck, she sighed against his lips.

"I don't ever want you to stop talking to me again," Aaron whispered.

Why would he say that at a moment like this?

"You were avoiding me," he went on, answering her unspoken question. "But I can't live without touching you." He smoothed his palms down her bare back. "Without kissing you."

"Aaron…"

"I don't want you to fight this anymore, that's what I'm saying. Why fight something we both want?"

Melissa pressed her body closer to his. "I'm not fighting…"

With a primal sound rumbling in his chest, he kissed her

again, ravaging her mouth with his. He slid his hands down and over her behind and pulled her against him forcefully. Melissa could feel the rock-hard evidence of his desire for her pressing against her pelvis.

She dug her fingernails into his shoulders and raised one leg high around his thigh. Aaron secured his hands on her behind and lifted her, and Melissa wrapped both legs around his waist.

"Yes, baby…"

Aaron's mouth widened, and he deepened the kiss, their tongues mating at fever pitch now. He moved with her swiftly down the hallway, and Melissa slipped a hand between their bodies. She tried unsuccessfully to undo the buttons of Aaron's shirt. Her concentration wasn't what it should be, not with his tongue assaulting her senses and making her body weak.

Aaron took over, and with one strong pull ripped his shirt apart. It was a shocking action, and one that stoked Melissa's inner fire even more.

Aaron lowered her onto the bed, his tongue still twisting hungrily with hers. Melissa pulled and pushed the fabric of Aaron's shirt off his shoulders, reveling in the feel of his smooth skin underneath her fingertips, and of his muscular chest pressed against her breasts. As the weight of his body settled on hers, he moved his lips from her mouth to her earlobe, suckling the flesh, and Melissa gripped his upper arms as the sweetest sensations flooded her.

Her earlobes were an erogenous zone, something she hadn't known before her night with Aaron after the wedding.

Aaron covered both of her breasts with his hands. He took her nipples between his thumb and forefinger at the same time, tugging on them both. They hardened instantly at his touch.

"My God, Melissa. Everything about you is driving me wild."

Aaron moved his mouth from her earlobe and brought it down on her breast. His whole mouth covered her nipple, and his tongue twirled around and around the tip. Melissa gripped his shoulders as her body was lost in a sea of intense feelings. Then he began to suckle softly, making her even crazier with need. She felt the heat and wetness pool between her thighs. She was ready for him. Ready for him to take her to that magical place once again.

He moved his mouth to her other breast and twirled the tip of his tongue over the nipple before taking it deep into his mouth and sucking hard.

"Oh, Aaron..." Melissa tightened her legs around his hips, urging him to be even closer to her. She needed his clothes gone and him deep inside her.

He eased himself downward and spread her legs apart. "I need to taste your sweetness."

Melissa's breath caught when Aaron dipped his tongue into her navel. Then his lips moved lightly over her belly as his fingers caressed her inner thighs. His touch was exquisite.

Aaron's lips followed the path his fingers had taken, kissing her inner thigh, close to her knee. Far from where Melissa wanted his mouth to be.

Slowly, his lips moved over her thigh, going lower. Melissa held her breath, and when his tongue gently flicked over her sensitive flesh, she expelled that breath in a rush.

"Baby!" she rasped.

Aaron's tongue worked magic until Melissa was panting and gripping the bedsheets. "Aaron...oh, baby. I need you inside me!"

Aaron eased backward and quickly pulled at his belt, then the hurriedly got out of his pants and shirt. Her body weak, her breathing heavy, she watched him strip out of his briefs from heavy-lidded eyes. The last time they'd been together, the room had been dark and she hadn't fully seen him. But now…*wow*. Her center throbbed at the sight of those washboard abs, his muscular biceps, his perfect thighs…

And his arousal—it was large and impressive.

Aaron Burke was the perfect specimen of a man. And he was going to rock her world again.

He lowered himself onto her and settled between her thighs. And the next instant, he was filling her. Melissa gripped his back as the sweetest sensations thrilled her body. Aaron groaned as he thrust into her, slowly and deeply. And then he went still, his eyes connecting with hers.

Melissa stared back unabashedly, her chest rising and falling with ragged breaths, something stirring in her soul. She wanted this to be about satisfying a sexual need, the most base of human desires, but she was feeling something else. Something that injected fear into this world of excitement.

She liked Aaron. As much as she didn't want to care about him at all, she liked him. And she knew in her heart that it would be easy to spend more time with him, make love to him over and over again.

And then what? He would destroy her again?

If he was the kind of man who kept his true feelings bottled up, it would always cause problems in a relationship.

Aaron lowered his head and captured her mouth with his. And as he thrust deeply inside her while moving his lips slowly over hers, Melissa stopped thinking negatively. She stopped thinking about anything other than the here and now, and how incredible she felt in Aaron's arms.

Each of his gentle thrusts was punctuated by soft sighs falling from Melissa's lips. She looped her arms around his neck and pulled him close, opening her mouth wide for him. She flicked the tip of her tongue over his, again and again, before locking her lips with his and kissing him deeply.

Aaron's hands tightened on her hips and he plunged into her swiftly, burrowing his shaft inside her. Melissa cried out, gripping him tighter. His body inside hers felt so good, so right. Aaron's body fit with hers perfectly, as though they were made for each other.

She pushed her hips up against his, urging him to go faster. He did. Together, the tempo of their lovemaking increased, until Melissa was crying out his name on a stream of erratic breaths. He kissed her jaw, her cheek, her earlobe, all of those actions adding to the exquisite sensations her body was experiencing.

Slowing the pace, Aaron eased his head back to look at her, and again, Melissa felt a charge. A sexual charge, yes, but something else, too. Something deeper.

It was as though the feelings she'd had for him, which had been buried for so long, were starting to escape the locked box in her heart.

"I've been thinking about this every day since I last saw you," Aaron whispered. "Of you and me, naked like this. All night."

"All night?" Melissa asked breathlessly.

"And all day. That's how much I love making love to you. For as long as we both need it. But I don't think I can ever get enough of this."

His words turned her on. Made her feel more desired than she'd ever felt.

Melissa wrapped her legs around him, holding him tightly against her. Oh, how easily she could make love to Aaron all day and all night. How much she wanted to.

And then he was kissing her again, his deep thrusts pushing her closer and closer to the edge. He trailed his fingers against the side of her breast, swept his tongue deeply into her mouth and burrowed himself inside her. The sweetest sensations began to build in her, and each stroke of his member, each taste of his tongue stoked not only her physical desire but something deeper.

Something emotional.

"Look at me, baby," Aaron said.

She did. Stared into his eyes and laid her soul bare. He held her gaze, and in that moment, she believed that there was something deeper between her and Aaron than just the physical act of making love.

She climaxed then, vaulting into that sweet abyss. Aaron kissed her as raw pleasure consumed her body and warmth filled her heart.

Chapter 20

Melissa's eyelids popped open. The room was dark, but she knew immediately that it was unfamiliar.

As was the arm draped across her naked torso.

Everything came back to her in an instant. The Waldorf Astoria. Aaron. Making love as if their lives depended on it.

They had barely been able to get enough of each other, sheer exhaustion the only thing forcing them to finally get some sleep.

A smile crept onto Melissa's face. The night had been incredible.

She angled her head, glancing at Aaron in the darkened room. She could make out his features, see his slightly parted lips, hear the soft inhalations of his breath. He seemed content.

And how easily she could be content in his arms. But there was that niggling fear.

Did he like her?

As soon as that question came into her mind, Melissa turned away from Aaron and frowned. Why was she contemplating whether or not he liked her? It didn't matter. She had spent these two nights with Aaron for one reason only—to scratch an itch. That had been the plan. Whether or not he liked her was of zero significance.

In fact, the goal was to forget about him once and for all. Clearly, she had a fierce attraction to him, but it was okay to be a hot-blooded female with desires. The time she'd spent with Aaron had reminded her that she was missing intimacy in her life. Why had she not yet set up a profile on an online dating site?

As for Aaron, hopefully after last night, she could purge whatever this was inside her that found him attractive and irresistible.

She glanced at him again, and desire spread through her body. The temptation to slip onto his body and wake him up with kisses under his jawline was seriously intense. Her mind and her body weren't on the same page. Her mind told her that enough was enough; it was time to be done with Aaron already. Her body, on the other hand, enjoyed every moment that he touched her, kissed her, made love to her—and wanted more.

And then there was her heart. It was telling her that what she was experiencing with Aaron was more than just sex.

The way Aaron held her, kissed her, the way he looked at her during the act of sex…it all felt amazingly intimate. Not like two people simply getting together to fill a physical need.

Don't go there, she told herself. Melissa couldn't get caught up in those feelings. She couldn't allow herself to believe that sex with Aaron was more than what it was. Obviously, a man like Aaron was used to having lots of sex with lots of women. He found her attractive; that was a given. And men like Aaron pursued attractive women and could have sex without letting emotions complicate things.

For Melissa to even begin to entertain any fanciful feelings that sex was more than just sex with him would be stupid.

He'd broken her heart once, hadn't he? She didn't want to give him the power to do that again.

She glanced at him again, thought of just how attentive he had been to her in and out of the bedroom, how great he'd been with the kids at the group home, and how much he cared about the Nunez family. He was a good man, one she could easily fall for again. But she had to remember that he had issues he hadn't dealt with, issues that caused him to shut down his emotions and walk away from her. He could easily do that again.

Melissa cared easily. She wanted to love without reservation. Give her body to a man who loved her from the depths of his soul. If she compromised on what she needed from a man, she would have to deal with the devastating consequences when she got hurt. She needed a man who was going to be open and vulnerable with her.

Even lying in bed with Aaron like this was entirely too comfortable, entirely the kind of thing that made her long for something more. She eased out from under his arm and slowly got off the bed. She was stuck in the past.

Because she'd never truly had closure on her relationship with Aaron.

She shook her head as she started to pad across the room, disappointed with the direction of her thoughts. She didn't need closure. She was over Aaron Burke. She'd gotten over him years ago.

Her dress was on the living room floor, where it had been quickly discarded when Aaron was desperate to get her naked. She wished she had something else to wear out of here, but the dress was her only option.

"Where are you going?" Aaron asked.

Melissa froze, surprised that he was awake.

She looked over her shoulder at him. "I was just going to use the bathroom and look for my clothes."

"And sneak off again?" Aaron asked, but there was a hint of humor in his voice.

"I probably do need to get back. I've got work."

"On a Saturday?"

"I typically go in on Saturday afternoons. I have some reports to do."

"We should have time for breakfast before you leave, then."

Did she want to extend her time with him? No. She wanted to flee. Even looking at him in the bed, his gorgeous body stretched out and the bedsheet carelessly strewn across his midsection, she felt her womb tighten with desire.

She wanted to stay here with him, make love to him over and over again, and forget the rest of the world existed.

Surely this wasn't normal.

"And maybe we could…one more time…" Aaron said, giving her a wink.

Her center throbbed. He hadn't spelled out the words, but it was obvious what he wanted. And good Lord, she wanted that, too.

Why was he so hard to resist? Shouldn't she be telling him now that this was the last time they could be together, that it had been fun while it lasted, but now she was going to get back to her real life in the real world and—

"Come here," he said, patting the spot she'd vacated beside him.

Melissa's pulse quickened. Then she did as he'd asked and made her way over to him. She eased her bottom down onto the bed, and he leaned forward and gave her lips a peck. "You standing there, naked, teasing me…it should be a crime. You know that?" He snaked an arm around her waist. "I can't get enough of you. Damn, girl, what have you done to me?"

Melissa swallowed. She wanted more than anything to believe that he'd never felt this kind of attraction for anyone else, that there was something special about her. That the sex between them was the best he'd ever had.

But she knew that was foolish.

She also knew that right now, she wanted nothing more than to have that one more roll in the hay with him. Before she went back to New Jersey and her life without him, she needed him one last time.

After making love once again, Melissa and Aaron had a breakfast of fruit, yogurt and granola while lazing around in bed. Melissa tried to keep a happy disposition, but everything felt bittersweet.

Soon she would be leaving Aaron, and this time she planned never to see him again.

But her heart was hurting a little over that fact. Their last time making love had been the most emotional of all their times together—slow, sensual and seemingly filled with meaning. Or maybe Melissa had felt more emotional intensity because she knew that she would soon be saying goodbye to Aaron forever.

There was no other way. She knew that. And yet, the idea that she was closing the door on him and what she'd once believed was possible made her a little bit sad.

Even more so because the sexual chemistry with Aaron had been all she could ever want with a partner. He brought her body to heights she'd never experienced. She missed kissing, making love, lying in bed with someone.

But she wanted that with someone in the context of a relationship—a real one. Not with someone who was good at scratching an itch, but not good at committing.

There was too much baggage between her and Aaron for her to believe he could possibly be the man she needed, even if on some level, somewhere deep inside her, she wished that he could be.

They'd had their chance, hadn't they? And Aaron had blown it. They hadn't talked over the years. Melissa had always believed that once a relationship was over, there was no going back to it.

She gazed at Aaron, who looked so darn tempting wearing only his boxer briefs, sitting on the bed beside her. She was wearing one of his T-shirts, which was huge on her. This was nice…and she would enjoy these last few minutes with him, then move on.

"I'd better get changed," Melissa said. Just as Aaron tried to reach for her, she slid off the bed, giggling.

Honestly, she knew that if she weren't leaving, she and

Aaron would spend the day here naked, making a love den out of this suite at the Waldorf Astoria.

Thankfully, Aaron had had the foresight to have her bag with her regular clothes sent up to the room, so Melissa didn't have to leave the hotel all decked out in her stunning gown. She was glad not to have to do that walk of shame. And the staff was nice enough to get her a hanger and a plastic dress bag to carry her gown with her.

A short while later, she was dressed and ready to leave. Aaron took her garment bag, and together they left the room, neither of them saying a word.

But once they were in the elevator, Aaron used his free hand to pull her against his body. He gave her a soft kiss on the lips. "I wish you didn't have to leave yet."

"You're insatiable," Melissa teased.

"You weren't complaining last night." He gave her another kiss. "Nor this morning."

She looked up at him, giving him a bashful smile. She hadn't been complaining, not in the least.

The elevator pinged, alerting them of their arrival on the main floor. With a groan, Aaron released her.

He adjusted the hanger with Melissa's gown at the back of his shoulder as the elevator doors opened. He took her hand and they strolled through the lobby. Melissa felt as though all eyes were on her.

The memory of Aaron's body tangled with hers caused a hot rush to pass through her body. Their time together had been spectacular.

Melissa glanced down at their joined hands, something she liked and hated at the same time. The hand-holding spoke of a level of intimacy between them, made her think that at least he didn't regard her as a woman he could just bed and throw aside. And she liked that.

But she almost wished that he *didn't* exhibit any signs

of caring where she was concerned. Because it would be that much harder to forget him.

They exited the front doors and walked out onto the street. Aaron walked her to the Maybach and opened the back door. He hung her dress inside, then dipped his head and gave her a soft, lingering kiss on the lips. "I had a great time last night," he whispered.

"Me too," Melissa admitted with a bashful smile.

"Maybe we can get together next weekend."

Melissa's heart spasmed. Next weekend? He wanted to see her again?

Before she had time to think, much less respond, he kissed her again, this time stroking her face as well. Tingles of delight spread through her.

Aaron groaned slightly, then released her. "Let me know you got home safely."

"Sure." Melissa got into the vehicle, a mix of conflicting emotions flowing through her.

She knew that seeing Aaron again would be crazy, and yet as the limo driver pulled away, she turned to look at him. He stepped into the road to get a better view of the disappearing car.

He waved. Melissa waved back.

This was goodbye. It had to be.

Chapter 21

"Well, well, well," Teresa said in a singsong voice, a huge smile on her face. "Someone had a great night."

"I *just* walked through the door."

"Yeah, and even your walk is different. Come on, tell me how it was!"

"Where are Mike and Ed?" Melissa asked, referring to the other counselors who were working today.

"It's a beautiful day. They took the boys to the park. I should have gone...but I figured this would be the only chance we had to talk. So come on, tell me *everything*!"

Melissa's face instantly flamed. She hoped her friend couldn't see the extent of her embarrassment.

But why should she be embarrassed? She'd had the best night of her life, hands down.

"All right. Let's talk in my office."

Teresa squealed and hurried behind Melissa into the office. Her friend's excitement had Melissa flushing hotly with the memory of last night. Every delicious detail flooded her mind...and a wave of sensations washed over her. Aaron kissing her, the way his fingers and tongue explored her body...

"Tell me!" Teresa said. "Because I can see it in your eyes. You're remembering some of the dirty details right now, aren't you?"

Melissa slumped into her chair with a satisfied sigh. "I had a great time," she said. "It was spectacular."

"I haven't heard you use those words about a night with a guy...*ever*."

Melissa remembered Aaron's tongue on her earlobe, and she had to make a concerted effort to push the image out of her mind in order to keep speaking. "I needed last night," Melissa admitted. "He's gorgeous. The evening it-

self was fun and meaningful. The fund-raiser had me totally emotional. It was such a wonderful gesture for the
Nunez family."

"Hopefully that little girl survives and does well."

"From your lips to God's ears." Melissa paused. "Honestly, I thought I was going to be in a room with a bunch
of snooty people. People with money to burn who show up
and pretend to care just to be seen on Page Six. But honestly, I couldn't have been more wrong. They were sweet.
And they really did care. I was moved. A lot of money was
raised, and it was a wonderful thing to see these athletes
giving back as opposed to being selfish."

"More points for Aaron Burke," Teresa said.

Melissa's pulse tripped. She wondered again if she had
judged him too harshly. After all, he had been wonderful
to her, hadn't he? But she didn't want to allow herself to
go there.

Teresa's eyes were dancing with excitement. "I am so
thrilled for you. When are you seeing him again?"

"I'm not sure that I am."

"What?" The look of shock that passed over Teresa's
face could not have been more intense. "Why not?"

"First of all, we live in different cities. That's the biggest hindrance."

"He lives in your hometown?"

"Yeah."

"So? He can travel, can't he? Obviously he's got the financial resources. If he wants to see you, I'm sure you two
can make it happen."

"I'm not trying to plan out this crazy life of fitting in
sex with a guy between work and my other obligations."

"What other obligations? Stressing over the headaches
that happen here? If anyone could use a steady romantic
partner, it's you. Have you looked in a mirror? You look
like a changed woman."

And how nice it would be to have Aaron as a steady romantic partner. Melissa could get used to spending nights with him. Enjoying breakfast in bed. But that was a fantasy life, a fantasy in her mind. It wasn't reality.

"Because I had a bit of fun, which was just what I needed," Melissa explained. "But that's all it was…fun."

Teresa frowned. "Why can't it be more?"

"Because," Melissa said succinctly, then sighed. "Listen, there's a lot you don't know about him. We used to date years back, when I was a teenager. And…he hurt me. We were young, I get it. Still, you know?"

"No, I don't know. I can't make sense of anything you're saying to me right now."

"He married my nemesis from high school. He knew how much of a headache this girl was in my life. And he married her. The one person who thought she was better than every other girl. The prettiest, the sexiest, the best, period. Aaron married her."

"But they're obviously not together anymore…because you wouldn't have slept with him. Right?"

Melissa made a face at her friend. "Obviously not. I would never get involved with him if he were still married to Ella or anyone else."

"So what's the problem?"

"I guess what I'm saying is we have baggage. Stuff I'm not sure I can fully overlook."

"Are you serious?" Teresa asked. "You used to date, what? Twelve, thirteen years ago?"

"Twelve. But the last time we talked before the wedding was eleven years, nine months and some-odd days ago," Melissa admitted in a soft voice.

"Wait a second," Teresa said, her eyes widening. "If you're still upset about a breakup from nearly twelve years ago, that means you never really forgot him."

"It means I don't want to make the same mistake twice. Aaron has a way of making you feel wonderful—but when he shuts down, it's awful. I don't know what I did wrong, if he suddenly thought I wasn't good enough for him—or if something else was going on. But he shut down, refused to talk to me and broke my heart." Melissa shrugged. "Some men never let you in, and I don't want to deal with that again. Besides, now he's famous and used to women throwing themselves at him. He'd probably grow bored of me."

"I doubt it."

"But do I want to take that chance?"

"Well, you seem to have put a lot of thought into this. I wonder why."

Melissa's stomach lurched at the question from her friend. Why, indeed?

"Because... I don't want to be a fool. I can be a modern woman and have a lover and not need a relationship."

"So you want him as a lover, then?"

"That's not what I said. I already had my fun. It's time to move on."

Teresa's lips twisted in a scowl. "If you say so."

When Aaron's phone trilled, indicating he had a text message, he quickly scooped it up and retrieved it.

Seeing Melissa's name on his screen, he smiled.

I meant to text you earlier. I got home safely but had to hustle to get into work, which is where I am now. Thanks again for a great night...

Aaron had hoped that she would call him, but seeing this message from her nonetheless lifted his spirits. At least she wasn't cutting him off like she had after the first time they'd spent the night together.

Though if she did, she'd be in for a surprise. He wasn't about to let her walk out of his life, no questions asked.

Not after the undeniable chemistry between them.

Aaron was well versed in the art of the chase, but he was starting to wonder if he was losing his touch.

He'd headed back to Sheridan Falls, leaving a full day between Melissa's text and him reaching out to her again. He called, but she didn't answer.

Aaron gave it a few more hours, and he called again. Again, she didn't answer. After that, he sent a text asking her to call him when she got the chance.

Two full days passed before she sent a text.

Sorry I haven't gotten back to you. I've been very busy. Hope all is well in your world.

Aaron frowned when he read it. This was all she had to say to him? His excitement over the idea that he and Melissa had been rekindling something quickly faded into confusion and disappointment.

Had she faked her attraction to him in the bedroom? No, that didn't make sense. What would be the purpose in doing that?

Besides, he'd been there. Nothing about her interaction with him had been faked.

In fact, the explosive sexual attraction between them was on a level he hadn't experienced with any other woman. Years ago, Aaron hadn't been ready for a relationship with her, but now they were both older, both more mature.

And he knew what he wanted.

Melissa.

He wasn't about to give up on her without a fight.

Which meant he would just have to up his game.

Chapter 22

"Come on, come on. Where's that paperwork?"

Melissa clicked through the various folders on her laptop, searching for the report from the probation officer. Why couldn't she find it?

"This is ridiculous," she muttered.

Teresa entered the office and drew up short. "Everything okay?"

"No. I can't seem to find the probation officer's report for Marcus. Did I misname the file?"

"It's got to be there somewhere."

Melissa pushed her chair back and stood. She blew out a frazzled breath. Why was she this upset? All day she'd felt a sense of irritation, and she didn't know why. Every request from the boys or her coworkers annoyed her today. And the argument between Tyler and Marcus earlier had really gotten on her last nerve. She'd yelled at the boys, and she rarely yelled.

On her desk, her cell phone rang. Melissa shot it a glance, saw that it was a private caller and decided to ignore it.

"Well, this might perk you up," Teresa said.

"What?"

"That was a delivery man at the door. He dropped off an envelope. It was addressed to the house, so I took the liberty of opening it. There are tickets to a New York Red Bulls soccer game."

"What?" Melissa asked, not understanding.

"There's a note from Aaron. He wrote, 'Since the boys are big soccer fans, I figured I'd get them tickets for a game. Enjoy. Aaron.'"

"Aaron sent tickets?" Melissa asked, and in that moment, she felt the chill on her heart melting slightly. A part of her wanted to smile. Had her irritation been caused by the fact that she and Aaron hadn't been in touch?

How crazy would that be, since she was the one who'd sent him a brief, carefully worded message, hoping he would understand that she didn't want to keep communicating with him?

And he'd given her what she'd wanted. For two whole days, there'd been nothing from him.

And now this…

God, why was her irritation fading away?

Melissa's phone rang again. Again with the unknown number.

Anyone who wanted to reach her for business would be calling her on the work phone. She let it ring.

"Can I see that?" Melissa asked Teresa.

Teresa passed her the manila envelope, plus the note from Aaron. Melissa was reaching into the envelope when her cell phone rang again. This time she saw her sister's number.

She quickly snatched up her phone, a bad feeling gripping her gut. "Arlene, is everything okay?"

"No, it's not okay," Arlene sobbed. "Raven and Dad… they're in the hospital!"

"What?" Her sister's words didn't make sense.

"Dad was driving, he had Raven in the car, and the police think he had a heart attack. Oh, God…"

Dread filled Melissa's stomach. "*What?* Is Dad…are they…" She swallowed. "Are they okay?"

"Dad's in critical condition, and Raven…" Arlene sobbed.

"What about Raven?" Melissa asked, her heart seizing.

"She's not seriously injured, and for now she seems okay. But Dad…you have to come home. Right now. We need you."

"I'm on my way."

* * *

Melissa had dropped everything and taken a taxi to the airport as soon as possible. Once she was there, she had been lucky enough to get a seat on a plane that was heading to Buffalo an hour later. From the Buffalo airport, she took a cab directly to the hospital. It took her just over four hours from the time she'd gotten the call from her sister to get to Sheridan Falls.

Four hours in which she had been terrified, her heart unable to deal with the reality that the worst might happen. While she hadn't spoken with her sister again—Arlene had been too much of a wreck—she had received texts from her letting her know that for the time being, nothing had changed.

As the taxi neared the hospital, Melissa's cell phone rang. She let out a strangled cry, then looked at her phone, praying her sister wasn't calling with more bad news.

Her shoulders slumped with relief when she saw that Aaron was the one calling. Not her sister or mother with bad news.

She swiped to answer her phone. "Hello?" she said, her voice sounding frazzled to her own ears.

"I just heard," Aaron said. "Where are you?"

"I'm in a taxi. I'm almost at the hospital."

"Okay, good. I'm almost there, too. Is there anything you need?"

"I just need to know that my father and my niece are okay," Melissa answered, her voice cracking. Though Arlene had said that Raven hadn't been seriously injured, internal injuries weren't always immediately obvious. What if she was bleeding internally and the doctors didn't know it yet?

"They will be," Aaron assured her. "I'll see you in a few minutes."

Melissa swiped to end the call and pressed the phone

against her chest. She prayed that Aaron was right—that her father and niece would pull through.

The moment Melissa stepped into the hospital's emergency waiting room and saw her sister with Raven on her lap, she burst into tears. Then she saw her mother, and Mrs. Winston, her mother's best friend, sitting beside Arlene and Raven. Melissa hurried through the waiting room and threw her arms around her mother when she jumped to her feet.

"Oh, sweetheart," her mother said and began sobbing.

"How's Daddy?" Melissa asked, reverting to calling her father by the name she had when she'd been a little girl.

"He's in surgery, sweetheart. He had a heart attack, plus he got injured during the crash. We're all praying."

"I've been praying for the last four hours," Melissa said, hoping that God had heard her. She couldn't lose her father.

"At least Raven is okay," her mother said and glanced at her granddaughter. "Thank God for that."

Melissa released her mother and moved over to Arlene, who had gotten to her feet and was still holding Raven in her arms. Melissa needed to see for herself that her niece was all right.

"Hey," Melissa said softly, and gently fingered the bandage on Raven's forehead. "You're okay, sweetheart?"

Raven nodded slowly. "But I have a boo-boo."

"I see that. Does it hurt?"

"Only a little." Raven's little face suddenly fell, and her eyes filled with tears. "But Grandpa didn't wake up. Is he going to die?"

"We're all praying for him," Melissa said, not wanting to lie to her niece. "We're going to keep praying, very hard. Can you do that, too?"

Raven nodded.

Melissa wiped Raven's tears, then turned her attention

to her sister. As their eyes met, Arlene started to cry. Melissa pulled her into her arms and hugged her long and hard.

"There's no word on how badly Dad was hurt?" Melissa asked.

"He's having open-heart surgery right now," Arlene answered before a wave of fresh tears fell down her cheeks.

Oh, God. This was worse than Melissa thought. The accident hadn't killed her father, but his heart might give out on the operating table.

"Melissa."

At the sound of Aaron's voice, Melissa's knees buckled. She turned, emotion washing over her when she saw him standing in the waiting room. He was like an anchor in a stormy sea.

"Aaron!" She rushed to him and threw her arms around him. He cradled her head as emotion poured out of her.

"Do you know how long your father's been in surgery?" he asked.

As Melissa shook her head, Arlene answered. "About three hours. That's too long, isn't it? They should have finished with him by now, right?"

Still holding Melissa, Aaron faced Arlene. "We have some of the greatest doctors in the country right here in Sheridan Falls. I know they're doing their best to save him."

His words seemed to comfort Arlene, and his mere presence was making Melissa feel marginally better.

But the fact still remained: her father wasn't out of the woods.

Please God, don't let him die.

Though Melissa told Aaron that she couldn't possibly eat anything, he left to go the cafeteria, promising to return with coffee and snacks. Melissa was pacing the floor, her sister sitting and cradling Raven, not wanting to let her go, her mother and Mrs. Winston holding hands as they prayed quietly.

Suddenly, it seemed as though all the air had been sucked out of the room. All heads raised in unison, looking beyond Melissa. She saw the look on her sister's face, the way her jaw tightened and fear flashed in her eyes. She pulled Raven closer to her body.

Melissa quickly turned, following her sister's line of sight. Her heart slammed against her rib cage when she saw Craig, her former brother-in-law, storming into the hospital waiting room like a man possessed. He was marching right toward them.

Arlene tightened her arms around Raven, a clearly protective gesture.

"Is she okay?" Craig demanded.

"She's fine," Arlene retorted.

"But she could have been killed," he shot back, the accusation in his tone clear.

"Please don't tell me you came here to pick a fight, Craig," Arlene said.

"Because of you, Raven was nearly killed."

"You need to leave," Arlene told him.

"Not without my daughter," Craig said.

Raven started to fuss. Melissa quickly stepped in front of Craig in an effort to keep her sister and former brother-in-law apart. "What are you doing?" Melissa asked him.

"Stay out of this." He glared at her, and Melissa was so shocked by the venomous look in his eyes that she reeled backward slightly.

"Craig, this is a *hospital*," Arlene said in a hushed tone. "You can't behave like this."

He took a step toward her, and Arlene quickly got to her feet and moved several feet away from Craig. He followed her. Melissa followed them both, again putting herself between Craig and her sister. "Craig," Melissa began, "I don't know what you're doing, but you need to leave."

"If you can't raise our daughter without always leaving her with your parents, then I will happily take her. With what happened today, I'm sure the judge will hear my petition for revised custody. I knew this was going to happen."

"You knew that my father was going to have a heart attack while he was driving?" Melissa asked, sarcasm dripping from her tone.

"He's an old man. And the point is, if Arlene were doing her job as a parent and not relying on your family so much, this wouldn't have happened."

"How dare you?" Melissa's mother said. She was on her feet now, her red-rimmed eyes flashing fire.

"You're being unreasonable," Melissa said.

Raven was crying now, full-out bawling. "Everyone's staring," Arlene said. "Craig, think about what you're doing."

"Give me my daughter." His words were slow, deliberate, his teeth clenched. "Or I'm about to give everyone here a show they won't soon forget."

Chapter 23

The moment Aaron rounded the corner toward the waiting room with two trays of coffee and a bag of muffins, he heard the commotion. His face narrowed in confusion. What the heck was going on?

And then he saw. Melissa, Arlene and Valerie were on their feet facing Craig, whose posture said he was enraged.

Aaron quickly placed the trays of coffee and the food onto the nurses' station and charged toward them. He immediately got in front of Craig, who was much shorter than Aaron. "Hey, hey. What are you doing, man?"

Craig scowled at him. "This is between me and my wife."

"*Ex*-wife," Arlene clarified. She was swaying her body from side to side, trying to calm Raven.

"Look how you're scaring your daughter," Melissa said. "You're out of control."

"You need to leave," Aaron said firmly. "I don't know what you're trying to accomplish, but this isn't the way."

"You think everyone has to listen to you because you're a Burke?" Craig spat out.

"I won't tell you again," Aaron said, and the resolve in his voice was unmistakable. It told Craig—and anyone within earshot—that he meant business. If Craig was here to do anything stupid, he was going to live to regret it.

"You'll be hearing from my lawyer," Craig said to Arlene, then turned and started to walk away.

"I already have primary custody," Arlene said. "And everyone here can see why."

Craig stopped in his tracks and whirled around, but Aaron was there, stepping into his path. "You're going to want to keep going," he said.

Aaron glanced at Melissa then, saw her looking at him with awe and appreciation. He gave her a little nod, letting her know that she could depend on him to handle the situation. Craig wasn't going to do anything crazy—not while he was here.

Surprisingly, Craig stood his ground, even though a security guard had just appeared in the waiting room. Aaron raised his hand in the man's direction, letting him know he had the situation under control. Then he narrowed his eyes at Craig. "I'll give you one chance to rethink your decision and turn around right now."

Craig looked up at him, then at the security guard. Finally, he gritted his teeth. But it didn't take more than a few seconds for him to turn around and stalk down the hallway toward the hospital's exit. Clearly he knew that if he stayed and continued to cause trouble, he would end up arrested.

"Why is Daddy being so mean?" Raven asked, her big eyes wet with tears.

"Sometimes Daddy gets too angry," Arlene explained, stroking Raven's hair. "But he's gone now. He won't be yelling at anyone anymore."

Once Craig was gone, Aaron asked, "What was that about?"

"Do you want to go get ice cream?" Mrs. Conwell asked, approaching Raven with her arms outstretched.

"Mmm-hmm." Raven nodded exuberantly, then went into her grandmother's arms.

"And maybe we can also stop by the gift shop and pick up a toy," Mrs. Conwell went on.

As grandmother and granddaughter headed down the hallway, Arlene faced Aaron. "I don't know why Craig feels he can behave that way in front of our daughter. Doesn't he realize that he scares her?" She blew out a frazzled breath. "He's angry because I got primary custody. And he's been making my life hell because of it. Anything I do, he finds fault with. Apparently it's my fault that my father had a heart attack while driving, and I should have known that would happen. He's angry that Raven was in the car instead of grateful that she wasn't seriously hurt."

"If memory serves, Sean Callahan was his lawyer," Aaron said, more to himself.

"Yes," Arlene said. "Word is, he gave Sean a hard time during our custody proceedings. He felt Sean was failing him somehow."

"That's no surprise." Given Craig's behavior minutes ago, he could imagine the man being belligerent with his lawyer when things didn't go his way. "Listen, Arlene. If Craig does anything that frightens you, anything at all, don't hesitate to call the police. In the meantime, I'm going to have a chat with his lawyer."

"You don't need to get involved," Arlene said. "I can take care of Craig."

"Still, I'll probably give Sean a call. See if I can gauge if he knows what Craig's frame of mind is. I don't like how he seems. Like he's off his hinges."

"I can't disagree with that," Arlene said.

"And you should alert the police to what happened here today," Aaron said.

Arlene made a face. "Oh, I don't know about that."

"He's right," Melissa said, coming to stand beside Aaron. "You need to make sure there's a record of what happened today. Maybe a visit from the police about his behavior is the wake-up call Craig needs."

Slowly, Arlene nodded. "All right. I'll call them."

When Arlene headed back over to her seat and slumped into the chair, Aaron put his hands on Melissa's shoulders. "Don't worry," he said to her. "I'll help take care of this. My dad knows the best legal people in the city and the state. Just make sure that your sister contacts the police. Craig needs to hear from them that he can't behave like this."

"You really want to help us, don't you?"

"Why do you seem so surprised?" Aaron asked her.

"I don't know." She offered him a small smile, and there was that look of wonder again. Was she surprised that he cared about her?

"I've known your family since I was a little boy. Of course I want to help. I don't want to see any of you hurt."

"I got the tickets you sent for the boys," Melissa said. "The package arrived just before I got the news. The kids will be thrilled." She exhaled a shaky breath, her expression twisting. "I'm so scared about my father."

"Hey," Aaron said, placing a finger beneath her chin and angling her face upward. "Have faith. The best team of cardiac surgeons is working on him. He's going to pull through."

And then Melissa laid her head against his chest, and he gently held it there. He wished more than anything that he could take this pain and fear away from her.

The best he could do was be by her side to help her through this. And that's exactly where he would be.

An hour later, one of the surgeons came out to the waiting room. Melissa, her sister and her mother gripped hands, waiting to hear the news.

"He pulled through the surgery," the doctor said, smiling. "We had to stop the internal bleeding from the accident, then do a coronary bypass to improve blood supply to his heart. He's very lucky."

"Can we see him?" Melissa's mother asked.

"Not yet. He's in recovery. But we'll let you know the moment you can visit."

The news was a relief, but Melissa knew that her mother wouldn't feel better until she was able to see her husband. Melissa felt the same way. She needed to see her father to truly believe that he was okay.

The neighbors had started arriving before the doctor had come out to speak to them, bringing cards and flowers and food. Even though there was a cafeteria in the hospital, the food kept coming. Casseroles, sandwiches, meat loaves and even some desserts. As one of the older residents of the town said, "You need real food, not that horrible stuff they serve in this place. When my Gerald was here for his operation, he complained every day that the food was going to kill him before the cancer."

Melissa was amazed—and touched. She hadn't lived in Sheridan Falls for years and had forgotten how the residents would rally around someone in trouble. She'd remembered the nosy ones, the busybodies, but she had forgotten the good hearts of the people in this small-town community.

They had brought enough food for a house party—and promised more. They wanted to ease the burden on Melissa's family so that they could concentrate all their energy on her father.

"This is so much food," Melissa's mother commented, looking around at the trays occupying the tables in the waiting room. "And I can't even eat much more than a bite. Not until I get to see your father."

Aaron had remained at the hospital with the family, a source of comfort for Melissa as well as her mother and sister. He seemed to realize that Melissa didn't want to talk. The stress of her father's situation had her silent and introspective, and he was respecting that.

Melissa looked around at the waiting room, filled to capacity with people. Some were eating the sandwiches and brownies, and they were chatting and laughing. It was all so surreal, as if they were here for a social call.

"I think I need to get out of here," she mumbled.

"Why don't we take some of this food to your parents' house?" Aaron suggested.

Melissa looked up at him. He glanced around the room, then back at her, and she realized that he'd heard her comment.

"Um, yeah," she said. "That's a good idea."

"We'll just grab what we can."

Melissa took two trays of fruit and sandwiches in her arms. "Mom, we're going to take some of this food home. I'll be back soon."

A short while later, they were in Aaron's car and en route to Melissa's parents' home. They were silent during the drive, but Melissa noticed that Aaron would occasionally glance at her. He was allowing her silence, though, and she appreciated that.

Twenty minutes later, the food was packed into the fridge and Melissa and Aaron were back in his car. When he didn't start the engine, Melissa looked at him.

"What are you doing?"

"Why do you keep running from me?" Aaron asked.

"I'm not running."

"Like hell you're not," Aaron said. "You've barely looked at me since I got to the hospital. I know it's a tough day, but it's more than that. I've reached out to you, and you've ignored me. I'd like to know why."

"You really think this is the time?"

"I don't like this…tension. I like you."

"You like a lot of women," Melissa found herself saying, not even thinking the words through before they fell from her lips.

Aaron made a face. "So that's the problem. You think I'm a player?"

"You owe me nothing, no explanation."

"Then you shouldn't be upset with me," Aaron said. "Yet you've been hot and cold."

Melissa's face flushed, thinking of how hot they'd been between the sheets. "This is…awkward. Honestly, I'm not really good at one-night stands."

"Well, it was two nights," Aaron said with a small shrug. "You think that was my interest in you? A casual fling?"

"I'm thinking that maybe you...you have a fear of commitment. You end things when you get too close."

His eyes narrowed as he stared at her. "Fear of commitment? I got married, remember?"

Melissa didn't need any reminding. She pressed on. "What happened with Chantelle...maybe you fear getting close to people. So you end things before you lose them."

"You're psychoanalyzing me now?" Aaron asked, one of his eyebrows shooting up. "Because from where I sit, you're the one who seems afraid to get close to me."

"How can I get close to you if you won't let me in? What happened with Chantelle could explain a lot. Why you've had so many women."

"So you're telling me that you're the type to listen to rumor and speculation. And now you've come up with some analysis to explain my bad behavior? Without even knowing if it's true?"

Melissa sighed softly. She didn't want to be doing this. She didn't want to entertain any conversation about Aaron and his past, especially right now.

"Not that I want to discuss this now, but I saw that interview Ella did on television about your marriage troubles. She said you were incapable of being faithful. Why would she say that?"

"Because Ella is Ella," Aaron said simply. Then he sighed softly. "But why did you sleep with me if that was your concern?"

Melissa said nothing. She didn't have an answer.

"This isn't the time to talk," Aaron said, "but I would like to talk. Whenever things settle down on your end. I'll be here."

Melissa nodded. "All right."

Aaron started to drive. "The tabloids said a lot of things about me, none of which were true. I want you to keep that in mind."

"Okay," Melissa said. She wanted to ask him why it mattered so much, but she didn't. Because she was afraid of the answer.

Players lied. That's what they did best. If she let herself believe the sweet things he might say, she would end up devastated. Especially if deep in his heart, he didn't believe that he deserved love. Aaron might never be able to give her what she needed.

Three minutes into the drive back to the hospital, Melissa's phone started to ring. She dug her cell out of her purse and saw her sister's face on her screen.

"Hello?" Melissa said.

"How far away are you?" Arlene asked.

"Not too far."

"Great," Arlene said, and Melissa could hear a smile in her voice. "Dad's awake."

Melissa ended the call and beamed at Aaron. "Hurry. My dad's awake."

Chapter 24

The next few days were busy and happy, with a steady stream of visitors making sure the Conwells knew they were loved. Melissa's father would survive, and for that she was extremely grateful. Her father, doing much better than anticipated, was discharged from the hospital and allowed to go home.

Aaron had been around, as had many other Sheridan Falls neighbors, but Melissa had avoided having any serious conversation with him. It was too much to handle with everything else that was going on.

A couple of days after her father was home and settled, Melissa headed back to New Jersey. She needed to get back to work and deal with some issues before she could return to Sheridan Falls.

She was in her office two days after returning to Newark when she saw her sister's number and face flashing on her cell phone. She answered right away. "Hello?"

"I don't know what Aaron did, but Craig is singing a different tune. I spoke to my lawyer, who spoke to his lawyer, who said that the police also spoke to Craig. He's apologized, and he's backing off. In fact, the judge is imposing a few months of lost visitation rights altogether."

"You're serious?" Melissa asked.

"Yes. I don't know what happened, but I'm so relieved. I did tell Craig that I won't keep him from seeing Raven. We had a family talk, and he apologized to Raven and told her that he was sorry for scaring her. Because she really was terrified. I don't know, Mel, but I'm cautiously optimistic. For the time being, at least, it does seem as though Craig has done an about-face."

"Wow." Melissa was shocked. Pleasantly so. "Well, I'm happy. I'm cautiously optimistic as well."

"My lawyer did tell me that it was made clear to Craig that if he messed up, acted like an idiot or threatened me in any way, there would be dire consequences for him in court. I'm not really sure what was going on with him, but he seems to have gotten the point."

Wonders never ceased. Melissa was curious as to how Craig had been so easily persuaded to do the right thing after the way he'd behaved at the hospital.

"I'm so happy for you, sis. How's Dad?"

"He's good. But he's asking for you. When will you be back?"

"In a couple of days."

"Good. It's been nice having you here."

"It's been nice seeing you guys more regularly, too, even if the situation right now is not ideal."

"At least Dad's pulling through."

"Definitely," Melissa agreed.

Learning that Craig had done a 180 in terms of his behavior, Melissa wanted to talk to Aaron. He'd promised to deal with the situation, and it appeared he had. She wanted to know the details.

So she sent him a text and asked if he could meet her when she got to Sheridan Falls the next evening. He agreed.

That night, Melissa got into town a little earlier than she'd planned, so she went inside the café to wait for him.

As she strolled toward the counter to place an order, she locked eyes with the attractive woman sitting at a booth.

Ella.

Melissa stopped midstride, wondering if she should turn and flee. The last thing she wanted was to have this meeting here with Aaron while Ella was present. Not having seen her high school nemesis in years, she wasn't keen on being under the same roof as her.

So she went up to the counter and ordered a coffee, then

took a seat on the opposite side of the café near the window so she could watch for Aaron's arrival.

Two minutes later, she sensed the person coming up to her table before she saw her. "Melissa," came the soft voice.

Her heart beginning to pound, Melissa turned her head. And there was Ella, standing beside her table.

"Ella," Melissa said with difficulty. "Hello."

"I heard what happened to your father," she said. "I'm glad to hear he's okay."

"Thank you."

Without asking, Ella pulled out the chair opposite Melissa's and took a seat. Melissa looked at her curiously.

"I hear you've been seeing Aaron."

Melissa's heart stopped. "Excuse me?"

"It's a small town. Word travels."

For a moment, Melissa didn't know what to say. Finally, she found her voice. "From what I understand, you and Aaron split over a year ago."

"After he disrespected me in every way possible," Ella said. "He was unfaithful, he mistreated me. He didn't care about my happiness."

Melissa glanced outside, uncomfortable. Then she looked at Ella and asked, "Why are you telling me this?"

"I know we weren't close when we were young, but that doesn't mean I want to see you get hurt. Aaron is very good at the chase. He's very good at smooth talking women, and of course it helps that he's gorgeous. Before you get too serious, you need to know that bedding women is a game for him."

Melissa raised her cup to her lips and took a hurried sip, scorching her tongue. She lowered the mug. "I can take care of myself."

"Can you?" Ella asked and gave her a pitying look. "I thought the same thing. I thought he loved me. But nothing I did was good enough. And the other women…oh, how you want to believe that Aaron will only have eyes for you, but you soon learn differently. The thing is, I always felt sympathy for him. I think I knew that all his womanizing was about his sister, Chantelle. He was always so racked with guilt over her death, it seems he did everything he could to sabotage the positive in his life. Including our relationship."

Melissa swallowed with difficulty. The mention of Chantelle was like a kick in her gut. Suddenly, Melissa couldn't discount Ella's words. Because this was exactly what she had worried about where Aaron was concerned—that he would never let himself truly love because he could never forgive himself for the tragedy that had cost him his sister.

"I thought having a baby would save our marriage," Ella went on.

Melissa's eyes bulged. "You—you were pregnant?"

Ella sighed sadly. "I was. He wasn't happy. The stress over knowing he didn't want our child…" Her voice trailed off, and she closed her eyes pensively. Then she glanced outside and promptly got to her feet.

Melissa followed Ella's line of sight to where Aaron was exiting his Mercedes.

"What happened to the baby?" Melissa asked.

"I think he knew he wasn't loved. I lost him. Aaron— he's great at making you believe the fairy tale. And then you're left with a broken heart when he's ready to move on." Ella threw a quick glance outside, then hurriedly said, "Think about what I said. I don't want you to get hurt."

And with that, Ella spun around and quickly headed to the door. Melissa watched her leave, then looked in Aaron's direction. He had just exited the vehicle, and the sight of him in jeans and a white dress shirt had her heart fluttering.

Would she ever be able to look at him and not have this reaction?

She doubted it.

Oh, how you want to believe that Aaron will only have eyes for you, but you soon learn differently.

Aaron saw Ella hurrying away, then looked toward the coffee shop with narrowed eyes. When he saw Melissa through the glass, his lips curled in a smile—and darn it, her reaction to him was instantaneous. Her skin felt flushed; she could imagine him kissing her, touching her...

But then Ella's comments got into her head. She had voiced everything that Melissa feared.

The door chimes sang as Aaron entered the coffee shop and headed straight toward her. His smile grew. "Have you been here long?" he asked.

"Just about ten minutes," she said. She got to her feet, and he hugged her. "But that's okay. I was early."

"I see you already have a drink," Aaron began, "but would you like something to eat? Maybe a muffin, or a sandwich?"

Melissa glanced in the direction of the menu on the wall behind the counter. "I'll have the lemon pound cake. That's always been my favorite thing on the menu here."

"All right. Sit tight. I'll be right back."

He made his way to the counter, and Melissa watched him. He oozed an easy sexuality. It didn't matter what he was wearing; he always looked as though he had stepped off the cover of a magazine.

Melissa noticed that other women in the café were also gazing in Aaron's direction. It was hard *not* to look at him.

And of course it helps that he's gorgeous...

Ella's words sounded in her mind, and Melissa glanced away. She thought about how easily he'd seduced her and wondered how many other women he had gotten into his bed just as easily.

A few minutes later, Aaron was back. He placed a plastic cup filled with iced tea on the table, followed by two plates, each with a slice of lemon pound cake.

Melissa dragged one of the plates toward her. "Thank you."

Aaron offered her a smile as he sat across from her. "My pleasure."

Melissa broke off a piece of the lemon cake, stuffed it in her mouth and rolled her eyes heavenward. "Oh, this is good. How can something so simple taste so fabulous?"

"I know. It's my favorite, too." He paused. "I'm glad you called. I've been hoping we could finally talk."

Melissa nodded. "Whatever you did to help my sister out, I wanted to say thanks. It sounds like Craig is really backing off, and that's exactly what she needs. What we all need."

"I'm glad I could help."

Melissa looked at him, frowning slightly. "What *did* you do? I mean, how could you so effectively have Craig changing his tune? I don't imagine you took him into a dark alley and beat some sense into him," she said, her voice trailing off with a chuckle. Then she asked, mostly in jest, "Did you?"

"Nothing like that," Aaron told her. "But let's just say I was aware of some issues that Craig had. It gave me some leverage to give to Arlene's lawyer."

"Oh?" Melissa sipped her tea, waiting for him to continue.

"Although this is a small town, some things do remain secret. The woman that Craig got involved with…well, she made some unsavory allegations. I know because a friend's sister was very close to Craig's secretary. The allegations had to do with a bad real estate investment, missing funds and Craig's possible culpability. The secretary moved out of town, but I was able to talk to her. She's willing to testify against Craig if need be. Craig was made aware of this, and he knows that if he plays unfair with Arlene and Raven, this allegation can lead to a charge. Which is the last thing he wants. So he's going to behave, knowing that the moment he steps out of line, it'll mean trouble for him."

"Wow," Melissa said. "That's crazy."

"Craig's the kind of guy who's been a bully all his life, gotten away with things, blamed everyone else for his problems. But he couldn't bully his way out of this one, and with actual leverage against him, he was singing a different tune."

"He certainly wasn't the best husband to Arlene. Sweet and charming at first—then he became a different person."

Aaron is very good at the chase. He's very good at smooth talking women... Melissa's stomach suddenly roiled.

"I'd appreciate it if you didn't say anything to Arlene about this. She doesn't know the specific details, just that Craig changed his mind. This being a small town and all, I don't want word getting out. But if Craig does misbehave in the future, there's a recourse. I'm pretty sure he doesn't want to face jail time."

"It's funny how self-serving people are when it comes to that," Melissa said. She took another bite of the cake and washed it down with the tea.

"Well, enough about Craig," Aaron said. "It's good to see you."

Melissa's heart fluttered. "It's good to see you, too."

"We never did get to finish our conversation," he told her. "About whether or not you believe every negative thing you've heard and read about me."

Melissa's stomach was tightening abruptly. She felt nauseous, unsettled. Ella's words were weighing heavily on her.

She glanced around the coffee shop, knowing that in a town like this, ears were always open for gossip. "I'm not sure that this is the time or the place."

"Then come back to my place with me."

Melissa's eyes bulged at the suggestion, then she whipped her head left and right, certain people had heard what he'd said. Soon, phone lines would be ringing, word would be spreading.

Hadn't it already? Given what Ella had said, and she hadn't even been at the wedding.

Hastily, Melissa pushed her chair back and stood. "I really ought to get going. I'd like to see my father."

She started to walk away. She needed to be away from Aaron to keep her head clear. She didn't want to be lured back into his bed—

"Melissa!" Aaron called, but she kept walking.

By the time she made it outside the café, Aaron was hot on her tail. "Melissa, hey. What's going on?" He moved to stand in front of her, blocking her path. "We were having a decent conversation, and now you're running again?"

"I just need to see my dad." She placed a hand on her belly. "And I feel a little nauseous." She closed her eyes as the wave passed.

"Are you okay?" Aaron asked.

"I don't know," Melissa said. "Maybe I haven't had enough to eat. I had too much coffee before I left Newark for the long drive here, I guess. I just… I just really need to get to my parents' place."

"All right," Aaron said, not pushing the issue, but looking at her with concern. "You're okay to drive?"

"Yeah, I'll be fine."

"Call me tomorrow," Aaron said.

"Sure," Melissa agreed. Then she quickly made her way to her car without looking back at Aaron.

Aaron stared at Melissa as she hurried off, his chest tightening. He hated the uneasy tension between them. His feelings for her had deepened more than he'd ever anticipated. He wanted to tell her, but every time they took steps forward, they hit a wall. Melissa seemed nervous, on edge, and he didn't want to scare her into running.

Did she not realize how much he cared? Heck, the last time they'd made love, he hadn't even used a condom. He'd gotten caught up in the moment, yes, but there'd been something else. A primal urge to make something real with her. He hadn't been consciously thinking about pregnancy, but he hadn't been afraid of the idea. He knew that Melissa wouldn't be like Ella, she wouldn't use a baby as a ploy.

There was something different about Melissa. Something innately good and honest and wonderful. She was the kind of woman he could settle down with. The kind who would be a good mother.

With what he'd been through, he should be terrified of the thought. But something inside of him that he couldn't describe told him that he and Melissa were destined to have it all. A life together, a family.

It was something he'd known in his soul when they'd first started dating.

He knew he had his work cut out for him, but he had to make her believe that, too.

Chapter 25

The next morning, Melissa got up and went downstairs into the kitchen. Her mother was frying eggs, and as the smell hit her, she had the sudden urge to vomit.

She clamped a hand over her mouth, holding her breath until the wave of nausea passed.

God, why was the smell getting to her?

"Good morning." Her mother looked over her shoulder and smiled brightly at her.

"Morning," Melissa returned, taking a seat at the table.

"I'm making your favorite," her mother said. "Sausages and scrambled eggs."

Just hearing the words made Melissa's stomach roil. Maybe she was coming down with something.

"I don't know, I'm not feeling that hungry. I think I'll have some toast. I don't quite feel myself."

Her mother looked at her with concern. "Oh?"

"I haven't been getting a lot of rest. There was a crisis at the group home, plus my long drive yesterday. I guess I'm not taking care of myself too well."

Her mother waved the egg-covered spatula at her. "What have I told you about taking care of yourself? If you're not healthy, nothing else matters. Look at your father. He didn't heed the doctor's advice, and he went and gave himself a heart attack."

"I know, Mom." Melissa rose and walked over to her mother, then hugged her around her waist from behind. "I love that you care."

"I'll always care. I'm your mother. A mother's job is never done."

As the smell of the food wafted into Melissa's nose, she once again felt that rush of nausea. She had to step back. "Excuse me."

She'd been planning to sit back down, but instead she headed straight for the bathroom. Her mouth began to water, that awful sensation that told her she was going to vomit.

And vomit she did. She threw up, retching painfully as what she'd eaten the night before came right back up and into the toilet.

When her heaving was done, she rose, ran the water at the faucet and drank some, then washed her face. She placed her palm on her forehead. Was she coming down with a fever? Had she picked up a bug? Or maybe gotten food poisoning?

Feeling better, she headed back into the kitchen. "Mom, is the kettle on?"

"Yes. You know I always have a cup of tea to start the day."

"Good. Any peppermint tea here? I feel like I need that."

"Your stomach really is unsettled, isn't it? I was like that when I was pregnant with you. When I felt sick, I craved peppermint tea. Certain smells got to me, too."

Melissa's hand stilled on the tea cupboard. Her mother's words suddenly dawned on her, as did a horrific possibility.

Pregnant? Oh, God, could it be?

No…it couldn't be. She and Aaron had only had sex a couple of times. Well, a lot more than a couple, technically, but still.

But still nothing, she told herself. *You know how babies are made. Of course you could be pregnant.*

They'd used protection only the first time that first night, going with the passionate flow the subsequent times. Melissa hadn't been thinking rationally; she'd been feeling.

Oh, God…

With that, another wave of nausea hit her, but this time it wasn't because of her stomach. It was because of the idea that she might be carrying Aaron's baby.

"I think it must be the flu," Melissa said, more for her

benefit than for her mother's. "Or maybe food poisoning. I had the leftover fish last night. You never know."

Her mother made a face. "I had the fish, too. I feel fine."

"Who knows what it could be?" Melissa commented.

"Sweetheart," her mother began, worry in her eyes. "You don't look too good. Maybe you should go back to bed and lie down."

"Maybe I should."

"I'll bring you the peppermint tea and toast."

"That would be great," Melissa told her. She turned on her heel and headed back through the house and upstairs to her bedroom. All the while, her mind was whirring a mile a minute.

Could she possibly be pregnant?

Aaron was starting to wonder what it was going to take for Melissa to get back to him on a regular basis. It always seemed as though they made great strides, only for her to pull back.

He'd made it clear that he wanted to talk to her about his marriage, clear the air. She told him she was okay with that. And then she never got back to him. He'd called her last night—no answer. His better judgment had kicked in before he decided to go over to her parents' house and knock on the door and demand to see her. Her father was sick, recovering. She had a lot on her plate. She'd come to town to see her family, after all. Not him. But he wanted to know that she was the least bit interested in seeing him and spending some more time together.

Aaron frowned. What had gotten into him? Whenever a woman had given him the hot-and-cold act in the past, he'd been able to walk away. But something about Melissa kept him wanting to bridge the gap between them.

Aaron drove to the center of town. He parked in front of the café where he and Melissa had met just two nights

earlier. It was his favorite spot, as it was for most of the lo-
cals. He enjoyed starting his day with a bagel and coffee.
Today he was back for a late-afternoon snack.

He put his hand on the car door's handle, looking out at
the street to make sure it was safe to open it. That's when
he noticed Melissa entering the drugstore across the street.
He opened the door, about to call out to her, but she hustled
inside the store as though on a mission.

Aaron decided to forgo the sandwich and iced tea for
the time being and head over to the drugstore to say hello
to Melissa. Maybe they could find a place to talk after
she was finished buying whatever she'd gone in there for.

He jogged across the street and went into the pharmacy.
He didn't immediately see Melissa down the main aisle,
so he took a few steps to the right and glanced down the
next aisle to see if she was there.

He spotted her several feet away, her back to him. His
eyes ventured upward—right to the huge sign that read
Family Planning.

Family planning? Suddenly, Aaron's stomach tensed.
Moments ago, he'd been about to approach Melissa. But
now he couldn't help wondering what she was doing in the
family planning aisle.

He didn't imagine she was buying condoms.

Aaron made his way down the opposite aisle, which he
could easily see over because of his height. Melissa's back
was still turned to him, so she didn't know he was there.
He watched, his eyes growing wide, as she put down one
pregnancy test package and lifted another one.

Pregnant? Melissa was pregnant?

With *his* child?

Aaron ducked backward when Melissa promptly headed
for the pharmacy-specific cash register at the back of the
store. He heard only Mr. Baxter, the pharmacist, conversing as he rang up Melissa's purchase.

"Beautiful day, isn't it? How's your father doing?"

If Melissa responded, Aaron didn't hear it. About a minute later, he saw her quickly snatch up her bagged purchase and all but run out of the store.

Melissa glanced around as she exited the drugstore with the white paper bag clutched in her fingers. She felt paranoid, but there was no need to be, was there? She hadn't noticed anyone she knew in the store, which meant that no one had seen her pick up a pregnancy test. She hoped that Mr. Baxter wouldn't call anyone to share the news of what she'd bought, though she didn't imagine the older man would be so inclined. Besides, Melissa was sure that it would be against an ethical code for him to do so, anyway. But this was a small town, and word spread like wildfire.

Still, Melissa walked quickly to the corner and turned left to where she'd parked her car. She used the remote on the key to unlock it, and the headlights flashed. She rounded the car to the driver's side and opened the door.

And that's when her heart slammed against her rib cage. Because striding toward her car was Aaron.

For a moment she couldn't breathe. What was Aaron doing here?

She offered him a tentative smile. He didn't return the friendly gesture. Instead, as he got closer, she noticed that his lips were pressed tightly together. Something was wrong.

"Aaron," she said feebly. "Hi."

Aaron headed straight toward her, not breaking stride. Was he upset because she hadn't yet called him as she'd promised?

"I'm sorry, I meant to call you to set up a time to meet. It's just…well, my dad. I'm spending as much time with him as I can, obviously. And… I had to come out and pick something up for him." Holding up the bag, she smiled uneasily, hoping that he wouldn't question her little white lie. After all, her father was recovering from major surgery, and medication would be par for the course.

When Aaron still didn't crack a smile, Melissa wondered what was happening. He soon filled her in.

"Are you pregnant?" Aaron's eyes bored into hers. "With my child?"

Chapter 26

All the blood drained from Melissa's head. Feeling instantly faint, she swayed unsteadily on her feet. Good Lord, why had he asked her that?

As Aaron's unwavering gaze held hers, Melissa didn't know what to say. She finally sputtered, "Y-you were *spying* on me?"

"I saw you going to the store," he said. "I went in after you to say hello. Imagine my surprise when I saw you picking out a pregnancy test."

Oh, God...

"Are you pregnant?"

How could Melissa get out of this one? This was the last thing she wanted to talk about with Aaron, and now here he was, demanding an answer.

"I assume it would be mine," he said.

"Of course it would be yours," she replied, thinking only of defending her honor. "I told you I hadn't had sex for several months." Then, realizing what she'd said, she tried to backtrack. "I'm not saying I'm pregnant. I think... I'm probably being super paranoid. I'm just a little bit sick today."

Aaron's eyes lit up, as though something suddenly made sense to him. "And in the café yesterday, too. You said you were leaving because your stomach was bothering you."

"I'm sure it's just a touch of something. Maybe I ate something that didn't agree with me, or I'm coming down with the flu, or—"

"You obviously think it's more than a touch of something or you wouldn't have bought a pregnancy test." Aaron paused. "That is what's in the bag, isn't it?"

This was a nightmare. She could lie to him, yet what

would be the point? He already knew. He was just asking to see if she would be honest.

This was the worst possible thing that could have happened.

"I'm gonna take the test, just to be certain. But I'm ninety percent positive I'm not pregnant," she said, chuckling nervously to give the impression that she wasn't worried.

Aaron didn't blink—and she could tell that he didn't believe her.

How could she blame him? People didn't buy pregnancy tests unless they thought they were pregnant, for crying out loud.

"And if you *are* carrying my child?" Aaron asked.

Carrying his child…just phrasing it that way made the situation even more real. *His* child. They would be tethered together forever.

"If I am…" Melissa swallowed, the very idea terrifying. She couldn't deal with this right now.

"Were you even planning to tell me?"

"Aaron, you're jumping the gun."

"And yet you're the one holding a pregnancy test."

This was too much. Him demanding answers, her barely able to deal with the fact that she might actually be carrying his child…

"I'm not trying to pressure you or anything," he said, his tone a little softer now. "I was just…it was like a kick to the solar plexus when I saw you picking up a pregnancy test."

"This is a shock to me, too. But I'm probably overreacting. I'm used to thinking about the worst-case scenario."

"So carrying my baby is the worst thing that could happen?" Aaron asked, narrowing his eyes.

She didn't need him scrutinizing every word she said. "I'm not saying that. I just…let me take the test first."

"You'll keep the baby, right?" Aaron asked.

"If I am pregnant, it's going to be my decision what to do."

Something flashed across Aaron's face, something Melissa couldn't quite read. Then he said, "Would you actually consider terminating the pregnancy?"

"It's very early, but I know that you understand I have to make the decision that's right for my life. I won't be forced to do something I'm not ready for."

"You can't terminate the pregnancy," Aaron said, his voice leaving absolutely no room for discussion.

Why was he saying this? Guilt? Ella had made it clear that Aaron didn't want children.

"Aaron, I'm not going to have this conversation on the street. I'm also not going to have you telling me what I can and can't do." Defiance crept into her tone, and she was glad for it. She needed some anger to help her stay focused. She and Aaron didn't have a relationship, and yet here he was expecting her to have his child if she were pregnant?

Perhaps he would feel an obligation to his child and want visitation on the weekends, summers with his son or daughter. She would constantly have to deal with a man who was not her partner… Or worse, he might try to force a relationship because of the baby, but how long would that last?

Oh, Melissa had done her best to tell herself that she could sleep with Aaron and not get emotionally involved, but she knew now that she'd been lying to herself. He'd always been the man she had wanted, but did she dare to trust him with her heart again? She had been crushed when their relationship fell apart the first time. If she allowed herself to fall for him again and it didn't work out, then what? Especially with a child in the mix. She didn't want Aaron to want her only because of the baby.

"…consult me," Aaron was saying.

Melissa realized that she wasn't fully paying attention to him. Her pulse was thundering between her ears.

"I'd like to go home now," she said.

Aaron was silent for a long moment as he regarded her.

"Aaron, please. I feel so overwhelmed right now."

After a moment, he nodded. "All right. But we're in this together, so I need you to call me." When Melissa said nothing, Aaron went on. "Are you hearing me? I need you to call me and let me know if you're pregnant or not."

"I doubt it, but—"

"Call me regardless," Aaron said.

She opened her car and quickly got behind the wheel. The moment she closed the door, Aaron tapped on the window. She didn't roll it down; she needed to get away. Aaron frowned, then mimed a phone call.

Melissa looked ahead and drove her car into traffic, not acknowledging Aaron's request.

Good Lord, she'd hoped to find out if she were pregnant and deal with the news on her own. Now Aaron knew it was a possibility. He was going to be waiting to hear back from her.

And he expected her to keep the child, no matter how it might affect her life.

Well, she wasn't going to have him tell her what to do. This was the twenty-first century. A woman was entitled to make pregnancy decisions for herself. And she intended to make that decision without any interference from a man who was incapable of committing.

Melissa couldn't bring herself to take the test until several hours later. Arlene had come to pick up their parents and take them to a park for a change of pace. Melissa had begged off, claiming that she wasn't feeling well.

Which wasn't a lie. Although now, besides the nausea, she also had a pounding headache. The reality that she could be pregnant was too much to contemplate.

With the house quiet, this was the time to finally take the test. Waiting wasn't going to change the result.

She withdrew the test stick and followed the instructions. And then she sat on the edge of the bathtub and waited.

The seconds that passed seemed like hours. Was the line going to appear telling her that she was pregnant or not?

Melissa closed her eyes and kept them shut for probably a minute before she reopened them, reached for the stick on the bathroom counter and held it in front of her. As she looked at it, her stomach sank.

Positive.

Oh, God, the worst had happened.

She was pregnant.

With Aaron's baby.

What was she going to do?

Aaron didn't sleep a wink.

He had expected a phone call from Melissa hours ago, but midnight had come and gone and there had been no call.

He was trying to bide his time and be patient, not aggressively tell her what she should or shouldn't do. Even though he knew that there was only one acceptable action if she were pregnant.

To keep the baby.

Something inside him had perked up when he'd realized there was a possibility that he might become a father. He didn't even know how Melissa felt about him, and yet the idea of becoming a father had excitement filling his heart. It was something he'd wanted for years, a little boy or girl to call his own.

Sure, the situation wasn't ideal, but if he and Melissa had conceived a child, he would see it as a sign from God—that God had forgiven him for what had happened to Chantelle.

Aaron swallowed at the thought of his sister and how he'd lost her. When would the pain truly heal?

He had to convince Melissa to keep the baby. She had

to know that he would accept all responsibility for their child without reservation.

He had the means to take care of a child. And it wasn't like they were two teenagers. He would give the baby all the love in the world.

Enough love to make up for his one fatal mistake.

And yet, Melissa hadn't called him.

Aaron realized when he felt the pain in his jaw that he was clenching his teeth. He drew in a deep breath and then let it out slowly. He turned onto his side and glanced at the bedside clock—5:14 a.m.

Given Melissa's track record of disappearing, she could very well be heading back to Newark today. Before she left, he needed to know. He would give her the morning to get back to him, but she had to know that if she didn't call him, he was going to go and find her.

He had to know one way or another if she was carrying his child.

Melissa's feet felt like lead as she swung them off the bed. She sat there for several seconds. Her hands sank into the mattress, and she squeezed hard.

She wished she had just woken up from a dream, but she hadn't. The dawn of another day didn't change her reality.

She was pregnant.

Every time she thought about the positive pregnancy test, she felt such disbelief that she could hardly accept it. She needed to do another test. But not in this town. Getting one here had been bad enough, and she wouldn't put herself through that again.

When she got back to New Jersey, she would verify the test. False positives happened every day, didn't they? Taking another test before accepting the first result was the smart thing to do.

She couldn't stay in her bedroom all day, so she got up

and made her way into the kitchen. Her mother was sitting at the small table, as was her father. They had teacups in front of them, and they both smiled when they looked up at her.

Melissa returned the smile, trying to forget her own dilemma. It was good to see her father sitting up and smiling. He looked so much better than he had right after the heart attack.

"You look good, Dad."

"I feel better, too," he said. "Almost like my old self."

"That's because he's finally eating the veggies I made for him. This morning, he had steamed veggies and some roasted potatoes. He didn't even complain when I didn't give him any bacon."

Melissa looked at her father in awe. "Wow. That's progress."

"I'm getting used to it," he said. "This low-fat diet nonsense. I guess it won't kill me."

"It's meant to keep you alive, actually."

Her mother gave her husband a pointed look. "See? I'm not the only one who knows what's best for you."

Melissa smiled and wandered over to the counter. She reached for a single-serve coffee pod, but her hand stilled in the air. She'd done some research on the topic of coffee and pregnancy, and the experts said pregnant women should limit coffee consumption to one cup a day. But why not cut it out altogether to be safe? She would have peppermint tea instead.

The thought made her realize something. If she were indeed pregnant, she wanted this baby. Very much.

"I didn't know what to make for you," her mother said. "But there are some potatoes and veggies left, if you're okay with that."

The potato idea sounded heavenly. Melissa needed as much starch as her stomach could take.

"Sounds perfect," she told her mother.

She ate, and the potatoes did seem to do the trick. Although she'd felt a wave of nausea earlier, she was able to keep her food down. Maybe whatever she'd been feeling wasn't due to pregnancy after all. Maybe her stress over her father's accident and Aaron had led to a false positive. The only thing she knew for sure was that she needed to have a proper test with a doctor to verify whether or not she was indeed pregnant.

She would do that as soon as she got back to Newark.

A few hours later, Melissa was packed and ready to head out. "Dad, please stick to the new diet the doctor prescribed for you. I want to see you around for a long, long time."

"Exactly," her mother said. "He needs to be here for the grandchildren you're going to give us."

Melissa stiffened, a chill slithering down her spine. Why had her mother just said that?

But as she looked in her mother's direction and saw that she was smiling at her father, she knew her mother hadn't had some psychic revelation; she'd merely said the kind of encouraging thing a person would say when one's partner was facing a life-threatening illness. *Stick around so that you can see your future grandchildren.* There was nothing suspicious about her mother's words.

But still, the comment held far more meaning now than it would have just last week.

Melissa drew in a breath to steady her nerves, then made her way to the sofa and leaned down and gave her father a hug and a kiss. Then she did the same with her mother. "All right, I'll be in touch when I get home."

"You sure you can't stay a couple more days?" her mother asked.

Suddenly, Melissa started crying. Her mother got to her feet and put her arms around her. "Oh, sweetheart. I didn't mean to pressure you. I know you'll come back as soon as you can."

"I need to take care of some things," Melissa said, trying to contain her soft sobbing. Good Lord, what was wrong with her? "I'll be back before you know it."

Her sudden outburst was proof that she needed to get to Newark and her doctor's office immediately. She was an emotional basket case.

She hoped that when she returned to Sheridan Falls, this burden would be lifted from her shoulders. That she would know, once and for all, that she *wasn't* pregnant.

Chapter 27

Melissa felt a modicum of guilt as she exited her parents' home and brought her bags to the car. She'd promised Aaron that she would be in touch. And now she was leaving without speaking to him.

She sat behind the wheel of her car and decided to send him a text.

I need to go to the doctor to get a proper pregnancy test. That's the smartest thing to do.

And then she backed out of her parents' driveway and onto the street.

About a minute later, she glanced in her rearview mirror. And her heart spasmed. Was that...*Aaron*?

It didn't take more than five seconds for her to realize that it was him. The Mercedes pulled out from behind and sped up alongside her. She glanced to her left and cringed. He put the window down and gestured for her to pull over.

She turned her attention back to the road, not wanting to stop. Had he already received her text? Had he been lying in wait for her?

Aaron continued to gesture at her, but she didn't engage. And then he sped up and pulled in front of her. Melissa gasped. She feared he was going to stop the car, but of course that didn't make sense. Several seconds later, the traffic light changed to red, and he stopped. She was forced to stop behind him, trapped.

Aaron quickly exited his car and walked toward her. He rapped on the window, and she put it down. What else could she do?

"Turn into the next plaza. We need to talk."

Darn it, there was no avoiding this. She could run now,

but he would track her down. And the truth was, she did owe him an answer. Perhaps he hadn't slept all night, just as she hadn't.

She pulled into the next driveway behind him, which led into a strip mall plaza. Aaron drove to the far end of the parking lot and parked his car. Melissa pulled up alongside him.

He glanced through his window at her. She looked back. Then he got out of his car, came to her passenger door and pulled on it.

It was locked, and Melissa quickly unlocked it so that he could gain access to her car. As Aaron got into the passenger seat beside her, his disappointment was clear. "You were supposed to call me."

"I sent you a text."

"I just saw that. You didn't give me an answer about the pregnancy test."

"I think it's best that I go to the doctor to have a proper test done."

Aaron was silent, his eyes scrutinizing her. "Does that mean that the test was positive?" he surmised. "Because if it wasn't, you wouldn't go to the doctor to double-check, would you?"

When Melissa said nothing, he nodded, convinced of his own assessment. "Yeah, that makes sense. You got a positive result, now you're panicking. And you were gonna leave town without telling me what was going on."

"Aaron, this is all so overwhelming. I need time to digest this. Time to…deal."

"You mean *we*," he said. "You didn't get pregnant by yourself."

"But I might not be pregnant. There's definitely a chance that the test was wrong. I think it makes perfect sense for me to want to validate it first before you and I have this conversation."

"Please tell me you're not considering terminating the pregnancy."

"I need time to figure out what's best."

"What's best is keeping the baby."

"Do you even want a baby?" Melissa asked. "You're a jet-setter. You've retired from playing, but you might end up coaching in Europe or God knows where. A child would cramp your style."

"That's what you think?"

Melissa sighed softly. "Look, maybe I shouldn't mention this, but the day we met in the coffee shop, Ella was there."

"Yes, I saw her leaving."

"Well, she told me a bit about your marriage. Specifically that you didn't want kids."

Melissa saw rage fill Aaron's eyes. "That's what she said?"

"She also said that you sabotage relationships because of your guilt over Chantelle."

Melissa saw the way Aaron's jaw flinched. But he said nothing.

"You're still not going to talk about your sister?"

"Chantelle has nothing to do with why my marriage to Ella ended."

"Doesn't it?" Melissa challenged. "It makes sense that you ended our relationship because you didn't think you deserved love —"

"I don't want to talk about Chantelle," Aaron said through gritted teeth.

"Ella said you didn't want the baby, and that you cheated because your guilt led you to destroy everything good in your life. If she hadn't mentioned Chantelle, I would have dismissed everything she said. But I know how much guilt you carried over your sister."

"It seems you've let everyone else talk to you about my marriage without giving me the chance. It's about time you hear my side."

"Okay," Melissa said softly. "I'm listening."

"I know it can be hard to ignore the crap you hear people gossiping about, or the stuff that's in the tabloids. But I'm not this playboy that the world thinks I am. Yes, I've dated my share of women. *Dated*, not slept with. But I've had a lot more women chasing me. It comes with the territory when you're a sports star. They all want something superficial. Bragging rights. A sugar daddy who will wine and dine them." He paused. "And that includes Ella. She lied to me from the very beginning."

"You must have loved her if you married her." Just saying the words left Melissa with a bad taste in her mouth.

"She told me she was pregnant." Aaron held her gaze, let that sink in. "Before we were married. We met up one time when I was in town, hung out a few times, and one thing led to another. I thought she loved me. But she had an agenda."

Melissa stared at Aaron, waiting for him to continue.

"One day she tells me she's pregnant. Far from what she told you, I was excited. A baby…it felt like a blessing. Like forgiveness for what had happened with Chantelle. I was determined to be the best dad ever. To spoil the baby and never let any harm come to him or her. So I did the right thing. I married her. It was quick. I was happy. Only after we got married, I noticed that she wasn't developing. Her stomach wasn't growing. She wasn't having any morning sickness. I asked her if we could go to the doctor, check on the baby's progress. Well, the very next day she came home crying, telling me that she'd had a miscarriage. Said she'd been to the hospital and the baby was gone. I asked why she never called me, and she didn't have a good reason, except to say everything happened so fast. I found that odd, but I figured it could have happened that way. Mostly I was upset she hadn't called me. I wanted to be there for her. Anyway, several months later I ran into her doctor. I talked to him about the miscarriage, and he was confused. In fact, he was confused by the claim of pregnancy altogether. And that's when I found out she'd been lying. She was never pregnant."

Melissa gasped. All this time, she had assumed that Aaron had fallen for Ella's looks and sex appeal. Instead, he had tried to do the right thing by her, only to find out he'd been deceived.

"You have no clue how much that hurt me," he said, shaking his head as his jaw tightened. "I thought she was having my child. I was excited about that. When she lost the baby... I felt her devastation, and I was devastated, too. Then I wondered if I hadn't done enough for her. Maybe if I'd gotten the help she'd wanted, this wouldn't have happened. The guilt I felt over Chantelle was back full force. I felt as though I'd failed Ella."

"Aaron, I'm so sorry."

"She wanted the status of having me as her husband and wanted all the best things money could buy. I gave her almost everything she wanted, especially after she lost the baby, because I felt guilty over what happened. Plus, she was so depressed and needed pampering. A trip to Venice with her best friend would perk her up. Or a shopping spree in Miami. Honestly, I felt like a fool. Once I learned the truth, I left her. That's when she started her smear campaign, so I didn't file for divorce right away. I wanted things to die down."

"You never said anything."

"Because I didn't want to lower myself to dragging her name through the mud. I always thought my character would show who I really was. But it appears I was wrong."

He held her gaze. Melissa's lips parted. "For the record, I never could wrap my mind around the rumors I'd heard about you—at least not that you would be callous with your indiscretions."

"There *were* no indiscretions," Aaron said. "I didn't cheat on Ella."

"What I'm trying to say is that I slept with you because… because on some level, I knew you weren't some heartless jerk."

"Marry me."

Melissa's eyes bulged. "What?"

"Marry me. I'll be there for you and the baby."

Was Melissa losing her mind? Certainly Aaron hadn't just said what it sounded like.

"There's no need for you to consider adoption, or God forbid, abortion…"

"I can't marry you," Melissa said.

"Why not?" Aaron asked, and the expression on his face said that he was genuinely perplexed.

"Because…you just got finished telling me that you wanted to the right thing with Ella, and how that turned into a big mistake. Now you're proposing marriage to me?"

Hadn't he learned his lesson? Marrying someone for altruistic reasons was doomed to fail. "I know you want to do the right thing, and I appreciate that."

"Are you saying there's nothing between us? Because this isn't like with Ella. We never had a meaningful relationship. I never cared about her the way I should have."

"And we have a meaningful relationship?" Melissa asked. Her pulse began to race. Part of her—a very big part of her—wanted to believe that they did. But the wall around her heart was so high, and she didn't want to get her hopes up.

"Definitely, we could."

Melissa's hope fizzled. "It has to be more than *could*. We can't just do something because I'm pregnant. This can't be about Chantelle."

As she looked at him, she also knew that he was proposing marriage not just to do the right thing, but because he didn't want her to terminate the pregnancy or give the baby up for adoption. She sensed that the loss of this baby would be as devastating as losing Chantelle. "Look, I promise you that I won't terminate the pregnancy. That's not something I ever really considered. It's not who I am."

"But adoption? You'd give away our baby?" The question sounded like an accusation.

"And your option is for us to enter a loveless marriage?"

He looked stricken then, and Melissa couldn't understand why. They didn't love each other. A wave of sadness washed over her with that thought. Her feelings for him had deepened. No doubt about it. Sex had clouded her emotions.

"I liked how things were developing between us," Aaron said softly.

"But we don't really have a relationship," Melissa countered.

"Because you keep pushing me away. When are you going to realize that I keep coming back?"

"For how long?" Melissa asked. "Because if you won't deal with the pain from your past, how long before you run?"

"How do you think I'm supposed to deal with losing my sister? I'm just supposed to forget?"

"That's not what I'm saying. But you have to let go of your guilt."

Aaron expelled a heavy breath. "I'm not going anywhere. I *want* to be a father."

"You're only suggesting marriage because I'm pregnant. I know we like each other, but it's nothing more than that."

"On your part," Aaron countered.

"Both of our parts." Aaron had never told her that he loved her or anything even remotely like that. He was only saying this now because he wanted her to keep the baby.

"We can make it work," Aaron said.

"I can't say yes to your proposal."

She swallowed, thinking just how surreal this was.

Years ago, she'd hoped that Aaron would propose to her. If things were different and Melissa believed that he loved her and this was a romantic proposal, she would say yes. In a heartbeat.

But this was a practical proposal. A solution to a problem.

"So you're not even going to consider it?"

"I know that we have sexual chemistry," Melissa said softly. "But love…?"

She looked into Aaron's eyes, searching for an answer. Perhaps he would refute what she was saying, prove her wrong. Instead, he looked away. She couldn't read what he was thinking, but she could see that his brain was working.

"Just a few weeks ago, marriage wasn't even a remote possibility for us," Melissa continued.

"I do have feelings for you. Very strong feelings. But every time I think we're making progress, you pull away."

Melissa sighed softly. She didn't doubt that he had feelings for her. Lust, attraction and, perhaps, respect. But love?

"I have a long drive ahead of me," she said. "I promise, when I get a test done at my doctor's, I'll let you know the result. But right now, I do have to go. Okay?"

Aaron looked at her long and hard. Then he finally nodded. "As long as you agree to consider what I said. I don't need an answer now or next week. Just…give it some thought."

Then he exited her car, and tears instantly filled Melissa's eyes. The only man she'd ever loved was offering her the one thing she'd always wanted—and she couldn't say yes.

Chapter 28

The next day, it was confirmed. Melissa was indeed pregnant.

She left the doctor's office and went to work, hoping she could escape to her office and stay there undisturbed. If she didn't have work to do, she would go home. She needed time to truly process this news.

When Melissa entered the Turning Tides group home, she could hear voices in the kitchen. She went straight to the office but caught a glimpse of Teresa in the hallway just before she closed the door.

Seconds later, Teresa was opening the door. "You sneak in like that without saying hi?"

Melissa burst into tears.

"Hey, what is it?" Teresa asked, gliding across the room and over to the desk. "Tell me."

Melissa wiped at her tears, then spoke. "I'm pregnant."

Teresa's eyes bulged. Seconds passed. "You're sure?"

"Yes. My doctor confirmed it."

"But you're not happy?" Teresa surmised.

"The whole thing is a mess. I wasn't supposed to get pregnant...how can I have a baby now? It's the wrong time."

"As a single mother, I can tell you that there's never a right time. You make plans, but life happens."

"I know," Melissa said. "And I really admire people like you who seem to be able to do it effortlessly without a partner. But this isn't what I wanted for myself."

"What does Aaron want?"

"He asked me to marry him."

Teresa looked confused. "But that's great...isn't it? I thought you had strong feelings for him."

Melissa scoffed. "It was fun, but it wasn't a relationship. He just wants to do the right thing."

"This is the twenty-first century. There's no need to get married just because you're pregnant."

"I don't want a man who wants to marry me just because I'm having a baby. I want a man who's crazy and passionately in love with me."

"Maybe you've been so busy running from Aaron out of fear that you're not seeing the truth."

"What would you know?"

"Look to your left."

"What?" Melissa asked, confused.

"Look to your left. On the wall."

Melissa did. And she gasped.

Because there on the wall was the painting she'd put a bid on at the charity auction. The one of the swan on a lake by Felix Virgo.

"What…when…how?" Melissa asked.

"This morning," Teresa answered. "The card's in the top drawer." A slow smile spread on her face. "It's from Aaron, isn't it?"

"Did you read the card?" Melissa asked.

"No. But who else would send it for you?"

Melissa quickly opened the envelope and pulled out the card. She opened it and read.

I hope this painting puts a smile on your face. You loved it so much, I made sure you'd be the one to have it.
Love, Aaron

"What?" Melissa asked, the word catching in her throat. When had he gotten this? They'd left the auction early, and she'd hoped to hear that her bid was enough. Now that she thought about it, had Aaron made sure to whisk her away to keep his winning the bid a surprise?

"You need to call him," Teresa said. "Stop being so afraid."

Teresa left and closed the door behind her. Melissa pulled her cell phone from her bag. She held it in her hands for several seconds before she finally made the call.

"Melissa," Aaron said without preamble. "What's the news?"

"I'm pregnant."

"You are? You're sure?" He sounded excited.

"The doctor confirmed it. So, here we are…"

"I'd like to come see you. So we can talk in person. When's a good time? Tomorrow? Friday, maybe?"

"Tomorrow I have to go to court. How about Friday?"

"Friday's good. I'll see you then."

"Aaron, wait. The painting. I…when did you get it? I don't understand."

"I bought it the night of the auction."

"You did?"

"I put down a bid that I was certain would win. I wanted to surprise you with it at the right time. Today seemed like that time."

"Aaron… I'm shocked. I… I love it. Thank you so much."

"You're welcome. I hope it gives you that sense of calm it did when you first saw it."

"Yes," Melissa said, surprised that Aaron remembered what she'd said about the painting. "It does. In fact, I can use a good dose of that calm right now."

"I don't want you worrying about the pregnancy, okay?"

"It's not just that. I have to go to a hearing with one of the boys tomorrow. I'm worried about him. I'm hoping the judge will have leniency on him and understand that his father not being around was a factor in him committing the crime. I'm hopeful, but I always worry. I know that Tyler has a big heart. He just made a mistake."

"I'm sure the judge will see that, too."

"I hope so." She sighed. "All right, so I'll see you Friday."

"Yep."

As Melissa ended the call, her eyes ventured to the painting. A smile touched her lips. She no longer felt as anxious as she had just an hour earlier.

Did Aaron actually care more for her than she wanted to let herself believe?

The next morning, Melissa was heading out of the house with Tyler and Mike, one of the other counselors, when she drew up short. She blinked, making sure that her eyes weren't playing tricks on her.

Indeed, they weren't. Aaron was standing outside a car in front of the house. When his eyes connected with hers, he smiled.

"Excuse me," she said to Mike and walked down the driveway toward Aaron. "Hey, what are you doing here? We said Friday, remember?"

"I know." He looked beyond her, toward Tyler, and waved. "I figured I'd come by and see if I could go to court with you. On Tyler's behalf. Speak up for him, tell the judge he's a great kid. That I'm happy to mentor him, if that's okay with you."

Melissa stared at him, unable to fathom what he'd just said. Then she glanced over her shoulder at Tyler, who was grinning from ear to ear. She faced Aaron again, confusion making her head swim. "You're saying you came here to go to court...for Tyler?"

"If that's okay," Aaron said.

A wave of emotion washed over Melissa. She couldn't believe it. He cared that much?

He must, because here he was, in Newark, prepared to go to court to support a boy he had met once.

"What you told me really got to me," Aaron said in a hushed voice. "A kid should have his dad in his corner. I can't understand anyone who would walk away from that responsibility."

His words hung between them, and Melissa knew that they were for her as much as they were about the situation with Tyler.

"I'm prepared to come back here…often. Not just because I want to see you, but because I'd happily spend more time with the kids. They're great. Every kid needs an opportunity to succeed. It's what we believed way back when, when we were counselors at that summer camp."

Indeed it was. A slow smile spread on Melissa's lips. This was the man she'd fallen in love with. The one who cared about others and was giving of his time.

The wall around her heart was crumbling. And she couldn't stop it.

"I'm sure Tyler will be elated. Just look at him." She glanced over her shoulder, saw that Tyler was still beaming. "I don't know if you'll be able to speak to the judge, but we'll play it by ear."

"If nothing else, I'll be there for him."

This wasn't grandstanding. This wasn't putting on some elaborate show just to get to her. What would be the point of that? To play with young Tyler's emotions to score some brownie points with her?

No, she didn't believe that.

"Tyler," Melissa called, turning to face him. "I've got something to tell you."

Considering Aaron had only met Tyler once, he wasn't allowed to speak on his behalf before the judge's ruling. But it didn't matter. The very fact that Aaron was here by Tyler's side had caused a marked difference in the boy. He looked confident and happy, like a totally different child. Perhaps that was why the judge decided to be lenient. Or maybe she'd already made that decision before today. Melissa would never know. What she did know was that Aaron being there for Tyler had changed something in the boy so profoundly that the difference brought tears to her eyes. It was as though finally Tyler knew somebody cared.

Yes, Aaron was a celebrity. But it was more than that. Tyler had held his hand and looked up at him with the eyes of a boy looking up to a hero.

To a father.

Melissa was deeply moved. She could tell that today marked a turning point in Tyler's life. Aaron being here meant the world to him.

The fact that the judge had been lenient was a bonus.

They left the courthouse, all of them excited about the news that Tyler would not have to go to juvenile detention. He would be able to return to the group home, and in a couple of weeks, he would go home.

"Aaron!" Tyler bounded out of Mike's car and toward Aaron as he exited Melissa's vehicle back at the group home. He threw his arms around his waist as though this was the first time he was seeing him.

Tears welled in Melissa's eyes.

"Are you coming inside?" Tyler asked.

"Sure. I'll come in for a little while. I can't stay too long."

"I want you to be with me when I tell everyone the good news," Tyler said.

"Absolutely," Aaron agreed.

"I'm gonna miss everybody when I go back to my real home," Tyler said.

"Sure you are, buddy. That's normal. But you know what's awesome? You can still visit."

"Are you going to visit me?"

"Tyler," Melissa began.

But Aaron cut her off. "I sure am. I'm gonna make sure you're keeping on track." Aaron affectionately rubbed the boy's head. "Is that okay?"

"It's awesome!"

They entered the house, and Tyler shared his exciting news with the other boys. Aaron was by his side the whole time. Melissa stood back, watching the very real bond between Aaron and Tyler, her heart filling with even more love.

"Hey, can we play a game of soccer in the backyard?" Tyler asked Aaron.

Aaron leaned over so that he was at eye level with Tyler. "Actually, I'll have to come back and we can do that later, okay? Right now, I need to talk privately with Ms. Conwell."

Tyler looked from Aaron to Melissa. "You like her, don't you?"

"Of course I do."

"You *really* like her," Tyler stressed.

Aaron chuckled softly. "Is it that obvious?"

Tyler nodded enthusiastically.

Aaron stood tall. "I'll see you later, okay?"

Chapter 29

"Where are you taking me?" Melissa asked.

"You'll see," Aaron told her.

"You were really awesome today," Melissa said. "Tyler was so happy. I've never seen him so genuinely excited and hopeful."

"I was happy to be there. And I meant what I said. I plan to come back and visit. I'd love to take the kids to that soccer game whenever works best."

Melissa noticed that they were heading in the direction of the beach. "Are we heading to Brighton Beach? I don't have a bathing suit."

"All will reveal itself in time."

Melissa sat back in the car, listening to the slow jams playing on the Bluetooth. Songs from twelve years ago, when she and Aaron were teens. She closed her eyes, getting caught up in the emotions that the words evoked.

And then he reached across the seat and took her hand.

They stayed that way as they drove, the music taking Melissa down memory lane. Several minutes later, Aaron pulled up next to a walkway that led to a stretch of beach. It was out of the way, not at all on the popular portion of the beach that people frequented. To the right was an older wooden house that looked like it needed a lot of fixing up.

Aaron put the car into Park and got out. Melissa looked around, wondering what on earth they were doing here as he made his way around to her side of the car and opened the door.

"What are we doing here, Aaron?" Melissa asked as he offered her a hand to help her out of the car.

"You'll see."

So she let him take her hand and lead her down the path to the beach. It was hard to walk in the sand with her heels, so she kicked them off and scooped them up. As they passed the tall thicket of grass, she noticed a dock come into view.

"I don't understand," Melissa said.

The house in front of the dock had been partially obscured by all the brush and the large wooden fence. Now she could see that the yard was filled with tall, unkempt grass. The house definitely looked abandoned. Certainly he wasn't taking her here.

The dock reminded Melissa of the one on Sheridan Lake where she and Aaron used to sneak off and kiss at night.

Was that what this was?

He took the first tentative step onto the dock, and, determining that it was secure, extended a hand to her and helped her onto it as well. He walked all the way to the end and peered out over at the water. Melissa followed him. When she reached his side, he slipped an arm around her waist and held her close.

"I remember everything about that summer," he said.

So that *was* why he brought her here.

"I remember how we always snuck out on the dock at night." He looked at her, trailed a fingertip along her cheek. "How we used to steal kisses under the moonlight."

Melissa's heart began to pound. She thought for sure that he would have forgotten all about that. It was so long ago.

Aaron released her and bent to roll up the cuffs of his pants, then he sat down and dangled his feet over the edge. He looked up at Melissa, shading his eyes from the sun. "Join me."

Melissa carefully held her skirt around her thighs and then lowered herself down onto her bottom. She slipped her bare feet over the edge as well, let them hang above the dark water.

"I don't want this baby just because I want to be a dad. Although, I admit, that's something I've wanted for a long time. But I want this baby because I want *you*." He took her hand in his. "Because I love you."

A shuddery breath escaped Melissa's lips. The wall around her heart had already come down when Aaron showed up this morning to support Tyler, and hearing him say he loved her caused a thrill to rush through her body.

"I know we never really discussed the past, and what happened. Why I let you walk out of my life. I hoped you would realize that I was a different person now, but you kept running." He paused. "I was young and dumb. I was afraid of what I felt for you at the time. I know that's not a great excuse, but then there was my soccer scholarship, and me wondering if things could really work out between us…"

"I would have done anything to make it work between us," Melissa said. "I loved you so much. But when you shut me out, I felt like you never cared about me at all."

Aaron stroked her cheek. "I did. I fell for you, too, Melissa. How could I not?"

"And yet you could walk away?"

"I have something to show you. Actually, come back to the car with me."

Melissa stared at him with curiosity. They'd just gotten here and started to talk, and now he wanted to go back to the car?

"Bad planning on my part, but you'll understand in a moment."

Aaron hopped to his feet, then helped her up. They walked the short distance back to the car, where Aaron opened the trunk. Melissa sidled up beside him.

"What do you want to show me?"

Inside the trunk was a large rectangular box. Aaron took out the box, closed the trunk, then opened the box on the trunk's smooth surface.

Inside the box, Aaron pushed aside wads of tissue paper,

and the edge of a painting came into view. "Take a look," Aaron said.

Melissa did. It was beautiful. The painting depicted a night sky with a full moon. The moon's rays were shimmering on the water below. There was a dock on the lake and two people sat at the edge, with their feet entwined as they hung over the edge.

Melissa's lips parted as she fully checked out the picture. It was a young couple, African American, their bodies angled toward each other. Even without being able to make out their faces, Melissa's beating heart told her what the picture was.

"Is that us?" she asked.

"Yeah."

Then her eyes widened as she saw the signature. "Wait a minute—is that a Felix Virgo painting?"

Aaron nodded, a smile on his face.

Melissa's heart slammed against her rib cage. She stepped fully in front of the picture, holding it up in the box to better inspect it. The familiar brushstrokes, the unique way that Felix put color on a canvas. The feeling of calm his paintings evoked.

But this was *them*. This looked like the lake in Sheridan Falls. This couldn't have been a random picture that Aaron picked up.

"Are you saying that…you had this painting *commissioned*?" she asked, her tone full of disbelief.

"You love the artist. So I found him. Asked him to re-create this picture for me. For us."

Melissa was so shocked that she couldn't even find her voice. Aaron must have done this before he learned she was pregnant. Tears sprang to her eyes.

"Like I said, I remember everything about that summer. The way you used to smile at me under the moonlight. The taste of your lips. The feel of your skin against mine. The way we used to tangle our feet together."

Melissa's blood was rushing through her veins at warp speed. This was…incredible.

"Look at the moon," Aaron told her.

Melissa had to wipe the tears from her eyes in order to focus fully on the picture again. She saw now that there was a small object in the moon. She looked closer, and realized it was a little angel. As she stared at the angel more fully, she saw that it had a little girl's face.

She looked up at Aaron, not understanding.

"Why did I let you go? You were right when you said that guilt affected my relationships. I didn't believe that I deserved happiness. I didn't come to realize that until years later, when I did some serious soul searching. But it was more than that. I was also afraid, Melissa. Afraid of losing anything I loved. That angel is my baby sister," he explained. "I asked Felix to include her in there, because…well, Chantelle is a big part of the reason I fell in love with you."

Chantelle, his sister who had drowned.

"That summer, I shared with you my deepest pain. My sister drowned. On my watch. I'd been in the house, and somehow she got outside. She got into the pool. When I finally found her…" He grimaced. "Well, it destroyed me. And for a long time, I blamed myself. I was able to lose myself in the world of soccer. It helped me to escape my guilt. But when it came to love…" His voice trailed off, and he shrugged. "Why would a guy who let his sister die deserve love?"

Melissa put the painting down in the box and turned to Aaron. She stroked his cheek. "Oh, Aaron. Of course you deserve love. What happened to Chantelle wasn't your fault."

"At the time, I didn't think I did. I blamed myself for Chantelle's death, and you were the only one I opened up to about what I was going through. You understood my pain, you understood my heart. The night when I told you, you hugged me and cried with me and told me everything would be okay…that's the night I fell in love with you."

A sense of awe and love and bittersweet emotions spiraled through Melissa. She remembered that night vividly. Aaron's body folded against hers, his heavy breaths, his broken heart. She remembered it so much because it was the night she had fallen in love with him, too.

"Did you really fall in love with me that night?" she asked.

"How could I not?"

"I fell in love with you that night, too."

It was that night that they had left the lake and made love on the shore. With all the campers sleeping, they'd found a secluded spot and consummated their relationship. For Melissa, it had been the most profound and wonderful experience of her life.

"Then you shut me out," she said. "You let me go."

"Because what I felt for you scared me to death. It was something I'd never experienced before. Something so powerful it scared me. And I doubted it. I questioned whether or not I even deserved it. Did I deserve someone as special as you? So yeah, a stupid young guy unable to deal with his guilt pushed away a girl he loved. But it was never because I fell out of love with you."

Aaron was staring into her eyes now; she could see into his soul. Good Lord, he was telling her the truth. All this time, she felt that their relationship hadn't meant as much to him, but it had. And she'd been so devastated by her broken heart that she had kept her walls up this time, not truly allowing him in.

Until now.

"Oh, Aaron."

"I'm sorry," he said. "I never meant to hurt you. But… I didn't know how to deal with everything I was feeling. You were the one good thing that came into my life after

Chantelle, and I ran. Seeing you again at the wedding, everything came flooding back. All of it. But I realized you had shut down emotionally where I was concerned. And when you asked me about Chantelle, it opened up old wounds and feelings I'd tried to keep buried. You accused me of still not opening up to you, and you were right. I've kind of been at war with myself over the past several weeks because of what you said to me. I wanted you, but I knew that meant I would have to finally deal with my guilt. Which meant admitting something I never told anyone about the day Chantelle died."

Melissa's eyes narrowed and her heart pounded. "What didn't you tell me?"

Aaron paused. Swallowed. "The day Chantelle died, the reason I wasn't paying as much attention to her as I should have been was because I was distracted by some girl. I was on the phone with a girl I liked, sweet-talking her, making plans for the weekend, while my sister got out of the house and into the pool."

"Aaron…" Melissa's heart broke for him.

"Now do you understand? Love and relationships for me were connected to how Chantelle died. I couldn't get past that."

"You can't live like this, blaming yourself for a mistake. It's not a crime to have been on the phone. It was an accident."

"I know that now. But in order to really forgive myself, I had to finally tell my parents the truth about that day. I told them a few days ago."

"And what did they say?" Melissa asked, regarding him tentatively.

Aaron's eyes misted. "That it was high time I forgave myself. That Chantelle is in a better place where she's happy. That they know she loves me with all of her heart and would never want me to be sad. And that one day, when I see her again, she'll tell me that herself."

"Aaron." Melissa's voice cracked. "That's the sweetest thing I've ever heard. Your parents really are wonderful people."

Aaron nodded. "They are. They never blamed me when it happened, and that's why the guilt was worse. Because I hadn't been totally honest with them. I couldn't bear to tell them the full truth at the time, but I knew I needed to tell them in order to finally forgive myself. That weight has now been lifted off my shoulders."

Melissa stroked his face. "I'm so glad."

A small smiled lifted Aaron's lips. "And now…" He put his hand on her belly. "You're carrying my baby. I want you, and this baby. Because I love you. I always have."

Tears streamed down her face now. No one had ever given her a gift as meaningful as the painting. Every doubt she had about him vanished. She believed, finally, that she meant more to him than she'd ever known.

She looped her arms around his neck. "Oh, Aaron. I love you, too. I didn't want to. But I think a part of me never stopped. I kept running from you because you'd hurt me so much…but now I'm through running."

Aaron swallowed, and Melissa saw his eyes mist. "I'll ask you again, sweetheart. Will you marry me? Make me the happiest man alive and be my wife?"

A smile burst onto Melissa's face, and happy tears spilled onto her cheeks. "Yes! Oh, Aaron, yes!"

And then he kissed her, one hand smoothing over her belly while the other one stroked her cheek. It was a slow and meaningful kiss that bridged the gap from the past, and paved the way to the future.

A future that would be filled with lots of happiness and love.

* * * * *

KIMANI™
ROMANCE

COMING NEXT MONTH
Available July 17, 2018

#581 ONE PERFECT MOMENT
The Taylors of Temptation • by A.C. Arthur

TV producer Ava Cannon is stunned to discover that the lover who briefly shared her bed is one of America's most famous sextuplets. But Dr. Gage Taylor now shuns the spotlight. As they rekindle their affair, will Ava have to choose between a game-changing career move and her love?

#582 CAMPAIGN FOR HIS HEART
The Cardinal House • by Joy Avery

Former foster child Lauder Tolson is running for North Carolina state senate, but he needs a girlfriend for the campaign. The ideal candidate is childhood nemesis Willow Dawson. To fulfill her own dream, she agrees. Soon, they're a devoted couple in public, but neither expects how hot it gets in private.

#583 PATH TO PASSION
The Astacios • by Nana Prah

Heir to his family's global empire, branding genius Miguel Astacio turns everything into marketing gold. Only his best friend's sister seems immune to his magic touch. Until Tanya Carrington comes to him to save her floundering nightclub. Miguel is ready to rectify past mistakes. But will he win her heart?

#584 UNCONDITIONALLY MINE
Miami Dreams • by Nadine Gonzalez

Event planner Sofia Silva is keeping a secret. No one can know that her engagement to her cheating fiancé is over. Until she meets gorgeous, wealthy newcomer Jonathan Gunther. When he invites Sofia to lie low at his house, their attraction explodes…but will her dilemma ruin their chance at forever?

Get 2 Free Books,
Plus 2 Free Gifts—
just for trying the
Reader Service!

KIMANI™ ROMANCE

Want to give in to temptation with
steamy tales of irresistible desire?

Check out **Harlequin® Presents®,
Harlequin® Desire** and
Harlequin® Kimani™ Romance books!

New books available every month!

CONNECT WITH US AT:

Harlequin.com/Community

 Facebook.com/HarlequinBooks

Twitter.com/HarlequinBooks

Instagram.com/HarlequinBooks

Pinterest.com/HarlequinBooks

ReaderService.com

**ROMANCE WHEN
YOU NEED IT**

PGENRE2017